UNRAVELED

An Inked Novel

K.M.Neuhold

SYNOPSIS

Clay:

My mind and body are full of chaos; the only time I can truly feel free is when my hands, arms, and legs are secured. Just because I want to be bound, able to give over my pleasure entirely to another person, doesn't mean I want to be controlled, humiliated, or made to endure pain. I'm a successful, happy, confident adult man who wants a lover to tie him up. Why is that so scandalous? And why is it so difficult to find? It doesn't help that I've developed a hopeless crush on my straight roommate. Maybe a fulfilling relationship isn't in the cards for me.

Max:

I'm completely out of control of my life. My ex is trying to take my daughter away from me... *again,* my dream of owning my own motorcycle repair shop seems out of reach, and somehow, I find myself a thirty-two-year-old man who can't afford to have a place without a roommate. So, it's no huge surprise that the idea of being given complete control over someone's body and pleasure is a major turn-on. I never had any inkling I might be into guys, until my best friend told me he likes to be tied up. Now I'm losing sleep, imagining him bound and begging for me. I can't figure out if it's just the kink or if it's possible I'm falling for him.

CONTENTS

Title Page   1

Copyright   7

Dedication   8

Chapter 1   9

Chapter 2   15

Chapter 3   26

Chapter 4   36

Chapter 5   46

Chapter 6   59

Chapter 7   68

Chapter 8   79

Chapter 9   90

Chapter 10   94

Chapter 11   104

Chapter 12   114

Chapter 13   123

Chapter 14   138

Chapter 15   149

Chapter 16   158

Chapter 17   169

Chapter 18   182

Chapter 19   189

Chapter 20   197

Chapter 21   206

Chapter 22	216
Chapter 23	220
Chapter 24	227
Clay	233
Chapter 25	235
Chapter 26	250
Coming Soon!	255
Chapter 1	256
More Heathens Ink	260
More by K.M.Neuhold	261
About the Author	262
Stalk Me	263

COPYRIGHT

Book and Cover design Natasha Snow Designs

DEDICATION

For Kael Stryker for lending me one of my favorite lines in this book. And to Sheena   for sending me tons of Shibari inspiration on demand.

CHAPTER 1

Clay

*B*alance the books for the month, double check enrollment figures and class schedules, check with Beck about picking up an extra class, start planning the end of season recital...

The list goes on and on, rattling around in my mind as I rush through my morning routine of shaving and styling my hair into a messy faux hawk. My body buzzes with energy I need to expel, which means I need to make time to dance this morning and ideally work in some yoga. Maybe I can get Beck to roll out our yoga mats in the studio during our lunch break today.

I bounce on the balls of my feet as I wipe down the bathroom sink and make sure all my personal grooming items are stashed away again. I'm nothing if not a thoughtful roommate.

With a towel secured around my waist, I step out of the bathroom and run headlong into a wall of solid muscle behind a soft, black t-shirt.

"Whoa, sorry, man," Max chuckles, his large, calloused hands wrapping around my biceps to steady me.

My heart thunders in my chest as I fight the

urge to fist the fabric under my palms and press the rest of my body against the huge, solid frame of my very straight roommate. I said I was a good roommate, I never said I was a saint.

"Sorry." I yank my hands back and tilt my head back to meet Max's friendly smile with one of my own. We're bros, no big deal I'm half naked and fighting a chub brought on by his spicy, masculine scent.

"No problem. You finished in there?" he asks.

"Oh yeah, it's all yours."

Max gives me a nod of thanks and claps me on the back hard enough to cause me to stumble. I swear that man is like Lenny from *Mice and Men,* a big dope who doesn't know his own strength.

In my bedroom, I toss my damp towel into the hamper and open my closet to pick some clothes to wear. I card through a few different V-neck t-shirts and past some tank tops, trying to decide.

When I get to the end of my hangers of clothes, my fingers brush the silky black rope draped there, and a hot pulse zips through me, causing my half-hard cock to fill and stand at attention.

"Down boy," I mutter to myself.

It's been *ages* since my ropes and bindings have had any use, hence my hair-trigger.

For some people, being tied up from time to time is a great way to spice up their relationship once they know and trust their partner. But for me, it's a necessity, a desperate and deep craving. I *need* to be restrained and give my pleasure entirely over to my partner. Not only is it the one-time my mind is ever quiet and calm, but it's also the only way I have satisfying orgasms.

Something people with serious kinks don't tell you often: they can be extremely inconvenient. I haven't had a boyfriend in years, and with my luck lately, it doesn't look like it's anywhere on the horizon. And letting a stranger tie me up and fuck me is far from ideal. And trust is just the beginning of the issue.

I force myself to release the rope and turn back to the task of picking something to wear. I ignore my aching erection and the drops of pre-cum trickling down my shaft from even a few moments of imagining my hands bound behind my back as a man licks me, drawing out my pleasure until I'm sobbing for relief.

I huff at myself in annoyance and grab the next shirt I touch to tug over my head. Next, I pull open my top dresser drawer and grab a black jock and a pair of leggings—my typical work attire—and finish getting dressed in a rush.

I step into the kitchen and take note of grime on the counter and dishes in the sink. I grab a fresh rag from the drawer beside the sink and sniff it to make sure it doesn't smell moldy. It drives Max a little nuts whenever he catches me sniffing the *clean* rags. But I don't get up his ass about any of his hang ups. Granted, I may have *a few* more hang ups than most.

I make quick work of the dishes, wipe down the counter, and then keep going until I've made sure every surface of the kitchen is spotless. Only then do I breathe a sigh of relief.

I put the rag in the laundry basket, and when I return to the now clean kitchen, I notice a full pot of coffee.

"Have I told you I love you recently, you sexy man-beast?" I call out to Max in a teasing tone.

"You're just saying that so I'll keep making you coffee in the morning," Max yells back from the bathroom.

"Oh baby, if you'd let me, I'd show you that you're so much more than coffee to me."

Max's deep chuckle echoes down the hall and warms my insides.

I met Max a few years ago off a roommate-matching app. I nearly turned around and walked right out of this place when I laid eyes on him for the first time. The last thing I needed was a meat-head roommate desperate to prove how straight he is at every turn. I wasn't going to walk on egg-shells or fake being straight. Unfortunately, I also needed a roof over my head, and he was asking for obscenely low rent for such a nice place.

The universe must've been smiling on me that day because, as it turned out, Max is *nothing* like I thought he'd be. Yes, he oozes masculinity from every pore, and he's a bit of a grease monkey and gear head, working at a nearby mechanic shop. But he's also funny and comfortable in his own skin. He has no problem taking and dishing out my flirtatious teasing. In no time at all, he became one of my top two favorite people in the world.

I fill my travel mug with coffee and French vanilla creamer and slip on my shoes.

"Don't forget you promised to pick up Gigi from school," Max calls out as I open the front door.

"I wouldn't forget in a million years, love. I'll see you later; have a good day."

Max

I smile to myself as I hear the front door close behind Clay.

A guy couldn't ask for a better roommate and friend than Clay Rollins. Not only does he help me out with my daughter, hell he's the reason I still have shared custody of my daughter.

To say Georgia was unplanned is the understatement of the century. I met her mother, Jessica, in a bar seven years ago. I was a twenty-four-year-old kid, drunk off my ass and thrilled to be taking a gorgeous woman home with me. To this day, I can't remember if I bothered to use a condom at all, or if it just failed to block the goal.

The next morning, Jessica was gone, and I went on with my life without a second thought.

Until four months later when she showed up at my door with a little round belly and an ultrasound picture. She told me she had no doubt I was the father and that she didn't want anything from me, she just wanted me to know.

It took me a few days to wrap my head around everything, but once I did, I knew there was no way I was going to have a child somewhere in the world I wasn't raising personally. So, I'd called Jess and told her I wanted to be together and raise our child.

That lasted one year before I realized that no matter how much I tried to feel something for Jess, I just didn't. There was no spark, no excitement, and almost no attraction.

But when I told Jess it was over, she did everything in her power to keep Gigi from me. Enter Clay. We'd barely known each other a few months at that point, but when he found out what was going on, he got his friend Beck, who is a kick ass lawyer, to save my parental rights.

I never had a best friend before Clay. That must be why I feel a little zap of energy. He's an awesome person, and I'm lucky to know him.

I finish shaving and brushing my teeth, leaving my towel slung over the sink as I exit the bathroom.

A few minutes later, I'm throwing my leg over my bike and roaring out of the driveway toward work.

CHAPTER 2

Clay

"Oh my god, my muscles are so tight," Beck complains as we work through our morning warm-up yoga before classes start.

"It's a bitch not hiding behind a desk all day, isn't it?" I tease as I bend forward and touch my nose to my shins in *Padangusthasana* pose.

"Fuck off pretzel boy," Beck tosses back at me, and I chuckle.

Beck recently quit his cushy job at his father's law firm to come work at my dance studio full-time and do legal work for the local LGBTQ center for teens. I was thrilled to finally have him here full-time with me. Up until now, I've been teaching a majority of the classes while he picked up an evening one a few times a week. I finally have a little extra time to stay on top of the business side of things, and with both of us taking on classes, there is the possibility for expansion in the future.

I don't remember a time when I wasn't dancing. My mother has innumerable videos of me in diapers dancing around the living room. She said I was dancing as soon as I was walking. It must be genetic because in her heyday, my mother was prima ballerina for The New York City Ballet. I was a surprise pregnancy, but she never called me a mistake. It ended her career, but she never once made me feel unwanted or unloved.

I was never into the hyper competitive culture surrounding a dance company, so I opted to spend my life teaching dance instead. And thus, On Pointe was born. I really should stop by and see my mom soon. I don't make it over to her house nearly enough.

"My muscles are tight because I spent all weekend moving furniture and lifting boxes."

"That's right; this was moving weekend. Are you and Gage all settled into domestic bliss?"

Remember how I said Max is one of my *two* favorite people in the world? Well, Beck is the other one. So even if I am a *tiny* bit jealous that he's fallen in love and now living with his perfect man, I'm also crazy happy for him because he deserves it. And if Gage ever hurts him, I'll break his neck. Which I kindly told Gage last weekend when we all went out to celebrate their announcement of impending cohabitation.

"We're unpacked and organized. I'm still trying to get his input on the decorations, but otherwise we're all settled in. I love knowing I won't have to spend another night alone in bed," he adds with a happy sigh.

Beck and Gage are the real deal, so it's definitely not a *small* twinge of jealousy I feel in the pit of my stomach.

I'm saved from having to respond by the arrival of a few kids in Beck's first class of the day. I straighten up and greet the kids and their parents with a smile.

It's just as well; I have a million things I need to get done before my first class arrives in an hour.

Pay rent for the studio, send reminders for late payments, call an electrician to look at the lighting in Studio One...

I sigh at myself as my brain buzzes. My morning yoga gives me a few minutes to peace, but not to the level I need.

I head into my office and find my phone on my desk with a message notification from Grindr.

HotStuff: Hey sexy

I roll my eyes at the greeting. Although, at least it *was* a greeting rather than just a dick pic. Not that I have anything against pictures of dicks; I love them as a matter of fact. But if I want to see a dick, I'll ask.

I click on HotStuff's profile to see his picture, and damn he's as hot as advertised. I can totally forgive a lame greeting for a face like that.

ForgetMeKnot: Hey :) you're pretty sexy yourself. So, who are you HotStuff?

HotStuff: I'm a fireman, and I'm *very* interested to find out more about your bondage kink. Let me take you out for dinner and drinks?

Ooo, a fireman. Maybe this day won't be so bad after all.

I pull up in front of Gigi's elementary school and park in the pick-up area to wait for her.

I switch my MP3 player to my special Georgia playlist and wait for the adorable little ankle biters to start streaming out of the building. When they do, I step out of the car and wave down the little doll with long brown locks and big blue eyes. She looks just like her father.

"Hi, Clay," Gigi's teacher calls and waves.

"Hi," I call back as Gigi runs toward me.

I bend down and open my arms for a hug. She leaps into them and squeezes around my neck as hard as her little six-year-old arms can manage.

I help her into the backseat of the car where she insists on buckling her seatbelt herself.

"Is Daddy working?" she asks once she's settled.

"He is, but he'll be home in a few hours. And in the meantime, I thought you could help me make dinner, and we could have a dance party in the living room. How's that sound?"

"Yes!" she screeches.

Max

The loud whir and clang of various tools permeates the garage. I'm elbow deep in an engine with some Disturbed playing from my iPod dock.

"Hey, bro," I hear my brother Tony shout over the noise.

I stop what I'm doing and pull my head out from under the hood of the car to see what he needs.

I look over and see him making a rude gesture, and then I catch sight of the beautiful woman in the lobby, and I roll my eyes at him. You'd think he was raised in a barn with the way he behaves toward women. Or maybe I'm the weird one since I'm certainly the odd man out in my family.

I get back to what I'm working on, and it's not long before Tony is beside me, elbowing me.

"Did you get a load of her? She's something, right?"

"Yeah, she's attractive," I agree mildly. I only saw her for a few seconds, but it's easier to just agree with him.

"She's more than attractive, she's the future mother of my children."

"You already have two of those, Tony," I point out.

"Third time's the charm." he elbows me again and laughs at his own joke.

"Hey, did you see the ten in the lobby?" my

other brother Gio asks from somewhere outside of my peripheral vision.

"Back off, I already called dibs," Tony warns.

"Like hell you did," Gio complains.

I grit my teeth as my grown ass brothers scuffle over a random woman like two dogs after a bone. They're after a *bone* all right, and between the two of them, I have no doubt one of them will get it. My mother always said no one can turn down a Moretti man, and to this day, I have yet to see her proved wrong. It would help my brother's egos though if it happened from time to time.

"Max, get up here," my dad shouts from the front of the shop, and I let out a huff of a breath. I'd love to get this engine finished sometime tonight, so I can get home to Gigi. Not that Clay can't keep her happy and entertained, but I only get a few nights a week with my little girl, I don't want to waste them elbow deep in engine grease.

I pause what I'm working on again and grab a semi-soiled rag to wipe my hands before heading up front to see what my dad needs.

The woman my brothers are still arguing over is at the front desk when I approach.

"What can I do for you?" I ask her, assuming that's the reason my dad called me up.

"This is Lynn, she needs work done on her motorcycle. That's your specialty," my dad offers with a clap on my shoulder before sauntering off to let me take over.

He's right; I live and breathe bikes. And if

it weren't for the mountain of debt I'm still sitting under, I'd open my own shop to work exclusively on motorcycles. As it is, he lets me handle any that come in. Unfortunately, they're few and far between as most prefer to go to the more well-known motorcycle garages around town.

I spend the next few minutes talking to Lynn—for the record, she's way too sweet for either of my brothers—and get the paperwork squared away.

"I won't be able to take a look at this until tomorrow," I tell her. When her face falls, I decide to play my trump card so she doesn't decide to leave a bad Yelp review. "This is one of the only nights of the week I get my daughter, so I can't stay late. I hope you understand?"

Her face morphs from disappointment to that gooey look all women get when they find out you're a dad who gives a shit about his kid.

"Of course, it's okay," she assures me. "So, you're a single dad?"

"Yep, just doing the best I can to make sure my little girl is taken care of."

"Aww." She puts a hand over her heart and looks at me like I'm the second coming of Christ.

"Well, I'd better get back to work. I'll call you once I get a chance to look at her tomorrow."

I get Lynn's keys and give her a friendly nod before making my way to the garage again.
I barely make it back to the car I'm working on before I'm caught in a headlock.

"Dammit, Tony, get the fuck off me," I complain as my brother's sweaty, greasy arm encases my neck.

"You thought you could just go up there and snake my woman?"

"My woman," Gio shouts a correction.

"Jesus, I was doing my job, you fuckin' mook. Now get off me." I manage to get out of his grip and give him a good shove. "Act your age, asshole."

"Oh yeah? Why don't you check my dipstick?" Tony quips back, grabbing his junk for emphasis.

An hour and a half later I finish up with the car I had to get done and make sure my tools are all put away. It's *finally* time to go home to my kid.

"Later, assholes," I call to my brothers as I exit the shop.

In the parking lot, I swing my leg over my bike, a Triumph Daytona 955i, and pull on my helmet.

The engine roars to life between my thighs, and a familiar thrill goes through me. Nothing like all that power harnessed between your legs.

In a few short minutes, I pull into my driveway beside Clay's sensible Honda.

I open the front door and am immediately met with a sight that squeezes my heart and brings a smile to my face.

Clay and Gigi are twirling and jumping around the living room while some loud, poppy song rattles the windows.

I freeze in place, unable to break the moment as Clay shakes his ass and then picks up Gigi to spin her around.

My little girl throws her head back and giggles; the sound is music to my ears.

As the song ends, Clay collapses onto the couch with Gigi still squealing with delight.

"Is it my turn next?" I tease as I finally step in and close the door behind me.

"Oh, I'll spin you right round baby," Clay tosses back with a bawdy wink.

I chuckle, and a little unexplainable heat licks at my skin. It happens every once in a while with Clay. I usually chalk it up to the warm, fuzzy best friend feelings I have for him. He's my buddy, my bro. What else *could* it be?

I know a lot of guys would feel weird about Clay's flirting, but that's just Clay, and I'm glad he feels comfortable enough to be himself around me.

"Daddy, we cooked dinner for you," Gigi tells me as she crawls off Clay's lap and bounds over to me.

"You *did*? What did you make?" I scoop her up and tweak her nose, drawing another peal of laughter from her.

"Meatloaf. I squished the meat between my fingers; it was so gross."

"It should be ready, if you're hungry," Clay pipes in.

"Starving," I agree with a smile, heading toward the kitchen carrying Gigi.

"How was work?" Clay asks as I set my daughter down next to the table and start helping him pull out dishes for us to eat from.

"Fine," I answer with a shrug. "My brothers were working my last nerve; it's nice to be home, away from all that oppressive testosterone."

"Hey," Clay protests.

"I meant that as a compliment. You're not walking around swinging your dick like a weapon."

"That's a bad word," Gigi points out.

"It's not a *bad* word, but you're right; it's a word you're not supposed to say. I'm sorry," I say while Clay chuckles at us as he fills three plates. "Thanks for picking Gigi up from school and watching her until I could get home."

"I keep telling you, you don't have to thank me for helping out with her. We've been living together how long now? I feel like she's my kid, too."

My heart swells at his words. He *has* taken care of Gigi as if she were his own since day one. Yet another reason he's one of the best people I know. Maybe one day I'll find a way to repay everything Clay has done for me. Hell, if I can give him a fraction of what he's given me, I'll be happy.

We finish eating, and I clean up the kitchen since the two of them made dinner. Although, I'm under no illusion that Clay won't be back in here in a few minutes wiping down the counters again and checking each dish I washed. When we first started living together, it drove me a little nuts, but over time, I've come to realize the compulsions bug him just as much, so I have some sympathy for him.

"Let me put the kid to bed and then we can catch a few episodes of GoT, yeah?"

"Of course," Clay agrees with a small smile that brings out a dimple on his right cheek. I'm not sure why I always notice little things like that about him.

CHAPTER 3

Clay

While I wait for Max, I pull out my phone and check for any new messages from my new fireman friend. After I messaged him back earlier, we chatted on and off throughout the day. He's been quite the gentleman so far. But, before we can get to the next stage of meeting face to face, I need to tell him about my *preferences*. More often than not, that's where things go wrong. If not on chat, then as soon as we meet in person.

HotStuff: I have a few younger siblings. They are from a second marriage, so they're a lot younger, and I don't see them much.

I find the response to an earlier question I'd sent him. He really does seem like a nice guy so far. Well...here goes nothing.

ForgetMeKnot: So...the whole bondage

thing...

HotStuff: Yeah, tell me about that. I'm *very* interested.

ForgetMeKnot: I'm into being tied up. In fact, I need it. But, I am NOT into pain at all. I don't want flogging or sounding, none of that shit. And I don't like any humiliation play. These are my hard limits, and I understand if that's not something you want anything to do with.

HotStuff: I'm down with that.

ForgetMeKnot: Seriously??

HotStuff: Yeah. I can get on board with those limits. Sounds fun. But I hope it's ok if I take you on a date before we get to the fun ;)

ForgetMeKnot: That's more than ok. *blushes* Friday night sound good?

HotStuff: Can't wait

"You must be talking to someone interesting with that big smile you've got," Max comments.

I put my phone aside and make room on my couch for him. "Just a guy."

"Oh, a gentleman caller?" Max teases in a high-pitched voice.

"Shut up." I give his shoulder a shove and try not to laugh. Laughing would only encourage him.

After a second, he sobers and gives me a serious look. "You're careful when you meet up with these guys from online, right?"

"Yes, *Mom*," I tease.

"I'm serious, Clay. You hear horror stories of bad things happening to people who meet up online," he presses.

"Maybe to teenage girls," I argue. "I'm a grown ass man, and I can take care of myself."

His words hit home a little more than I like, though. Ever since I told Beck about my bondage kink, he's been on me to be more careful about who I meet up with. I know I'm putting myself in a vulnerable position, and frankly, I don't like it any more than he does. But a guy has needs, and dammit if I don't need a big, gorgeous man to tie me up and edge me until I lose my mind.

"Clay." Max reaches out and touches my arm, genuine concern shining in his eyes. "Please try to be safe."

"I promise."

Seeming satisfied with that, Max settles back on the couch, and I do the same.

The heat rolling off Max's large body surrounds me and beckons me closer. I want to curl up against him and feel his strong arms around me. All that stuff about Max worrying about me hit a place deep in my heart I don't like to think about. I don't need Max to take care of me, but no matter how many times I've told him that, it seems like he just can't help himself. He's a worrier. Not like me, my worries are more compulsive. Max is a natural protector.

Max turns his head and smiles at me. I blush

as I realize I've been staring at him for a good minute at least. In my defense, he's difficult to avoid staring at. He's so sexy with his long, dark hair, his captivating hazel eyes, and his always soft and welcoming smile. I can't think of anything I wouldn't give to run my tongue all over Max's naked body. And he's so big, I'm sure that task alone could take hours. But, I think Beck was way off base suggesting that Max is anything but straight. In the years I've known Max, he's never given any indication he's even curious. I've seen him date women, I've heard him have sex with women, and I've *never* seen him give a man a second glance.

Max's heavy head drops onto my shoulder, and his breathing gets a little deeper.

"Hey, I'm not a pillow," I complain, even though I'm more than happy to be anything Max needs from me.

"I'm not sleeping, I'm resting my eyes, and you have a comfortable shoulder."

I sigh but let him be. I get why Beck would take something like this to mean Max isn't straight. After all, straight guys aren't usually this comfortable with physical contact with other men, but that's just Max.

I allow myself one more quick second to appreciate his olive skin and tangled mane of black hair. I heard one girl call him an Italian Stallion after a night together, and I haven't been able to stop wondering if she was referring to his stamina or size...or both? In my private fantasy, it's definitely both.

After one episode, Max is snoring loudly in my ear and completely plastered against me, so I shut off the TV and give him a little shake.

"Time for bed."

Max mumbles something in his sleep and nuzzles his face into the crook of my neck. Goosebumps erupt all over my skin, and my dick decides this is the perfect time to sit up and take notice of the proximity of the masculine hunk currently lying nearly on top of me.

"Max," I grit his name out and try to push him off me, but that only makes the situation worse with him outweighing me by at least a hundred pounds.

Max's slumps against me, and somehow, I end up with one of my arms wedged under me and the other pinned beneath Max. I'm well and truly unable to move, and now, my dick is even more excited.

Fuck, this is so not the time for this. But my body doesn't care. My cock is at full mast now, my balls already full and heavy as all the signals register that I'm completely helpless. My heart flutters with excitement as Max settles his weight even more fully against me. That's when I feel it...his own monstrous erection pressing into my hip.

I was either very good or very bad in a past life to deserve this.

Max mutters something unintelligible again

and flexes his hips, rubbing his erection against me as I lay helpless beneath him. My gut tightens, and I squeeze my eyes shut tight, willing myself not to cream my pants.

It's been way too long since I've gotten any real action. Jerking off isn't even something I bother with most of the time because without being tied up and edged, the orgasms are never very satisfying so it's not worth the energy.

"Max, please wake up," I plead in a hoarse voice.

I'll never forgive myself if I repay Max's friendship by coming in my pants while he's asleep on me.

"Hm?" Max grunts, his head jerking up.

I let out a relieved breath, but then I realize I still have the very real problem of being so turned on I can hardly think straight.

"Get off me, please," I whimper.

Max rolls off the couch onto the floor in a flash.

"Oh my god, did I hurt you?" he asks in a panic, finally awake enough to notice my distress.

"I'm fine," I lie, tugging my shirt down to hide my erection.

Even if Max has one too, his was because he was asleep. Besides, I'm the gay roommate; if things get weird it'll be because I'm freaking him out.

"Are you sure?" he asks in a concerned stupor, still trying to shake off sleep.

"Yeah, I'm going to bed. Night." I jump up and scurry down the hallway as quickly as I can.

Max

Several minutes later, I'm still sitting on the floor staring down the hallway toward Clay's room. I'm not entirely sure what happened or why I woke up with a raging erection.

I'm assuming I fell asleep on Clay, but that doesn't explain why he was so freaked out. Oh god, what if I did something weird in my sleep like grope him or something? My gut twists at the thought of doing anything to hurt or upset Clay.

I finally get to my feet and start toward Clay's room, unsure what I'm going to say, but knowing I need to apologize.

"Daddy?" Gigi whimpers, and I stop in my tracks, immediately turning toward her room.

"What's wrong, sweetie?" I ask.

"I had a bad dream. Can I come sleep with you?"

"Of course, come on." I pick her up and carry her to my room where I change into my pajamas and climb into bed with her. As much as I hate letting it drop for now, apologizing to Clay will have to wait until the morning.

I rub my bleary eyes as the bed jostles next to me with the unmistakable motions of a six-year-old trying to be stealthy as she climbs out of bed.

It takes me a few minutes to drag myself out of bed and follow the sound of little feet to the kitchen where I find both Gigi and Clay at the table, each with a bowl of cereal in front of them.

"Morning," Clay greets me with a tight smile, only giving me a brief flicker of eye contact before focusing back on his breakfast.

"Morning," I grunt back as I make a beeline for the coffee maker. "Thanks for making coffee," I call over my shoulder.

"No problem." Clay's response holds none of its usual flirtation or playfulness, and now I'm really starting to worry about what I might've done to him last night.

"When you're finished eating, G, why don't you go get dressed for school," I suggest.

"I'm done, Daddy," she says, pushing her bowl away and climbing out of her chair to head to her room to pick out clothes.

"Clay, listen, I'm not sure what I did last night, but I'm so sorry."

"You didn't do anything," Clay says, reaching out and patting my hand in an unconvincing way.

"Then why are you being so weird?" I challenge.

"Can we please drop this?"

"You're my best friend; if I did something to make you uncomfortable— even in my sleep— I want to know about it."

Clay lets out a huff of what I can only interpret as annoyance, and then he stands abruptly, taking both his and Gigi's cereal bowls to the sink to wash.

"Clay."

"I got excited, okay?" Clay finally snaps with his back toward me while he scrubs the bowls.

"What?"

The water shuts off, and Clay spins to face me with a look of shame and anger in his eyes.

"You were on top of me, and I could feel your erection..." he trails off as the pieces click into place.

I wait for a second, expecting disgust or awkwardness to seep through me, but all I feel is flattered and maybe a little smug.

"How excited are we talking? Did you jizz your pants or what?" I ask with a teasing smile.

"I hate you right now." Clay tries to storm past me, but I catch his arm.

"I'm sorry; I shouldn't tease you. I swear, it's not a big deal. It's a biological reaction; it's not like it means anything."

"Yeah," Clay mumbles, still avoiding my gaze.

"Please don't let something like one little boner make our friendship awkward."

"Hey, my boner is not little," Clay protests. "And I'll whip it out right now to show you if I have to."

"I'd prefer to save any dick measuring contests for after I've had my coffee."

Clay softens and lets a laugh escape. "No need to measure, I could tell last night that you're packing serious heat."

Under the teasing tone, I detect a hidden longing, and to my surprise, heat spikes in my veins and my cock shifts in the confines of my pants.

I clear my throat and move around in my seat to make sure my sudden, random erection isn't visible. That happens to guys all the time, unexplainable hard-ons. It happens a lot less now that I'm not a teenager, but it's still not *that* weird.

"Are we cool, then?" I check.

"Yeah, we're cool. Sorry to make things weird, I just didn't want you to feel like I was perving on you or anything."

"Clay, you're my bro; I know you would never perv on me."

"Yeah," Clay agrees quietly before giving me a quick, forced smile. "I'd better go get dressed. Do you need me to drop Gigi at school or do you have her?"

"I've got her, thanks."

CHAPTER 4

Clay

I walk into my office at On Pointe and almost immediately turn around and walk back out. Even after my talk with Max this morning, my nerves are still on edge and seeing mountains of paperwork isn't helping. I rub my temples to try to ease the buzzing edginess in my brain. There are too many things on my plate right now, and I can't focus.

"Hey, you okay?" I hear Beck's voice behind me.

"Not really. I'm a bit overwhelmed. I have too much to do and no idea when I'll make time to get it all done."

"All right." Beck's places his hand right between my shoulder blades and starts to rub in concentric circles. "What all do you need to get done?"

"That stack of paperwork." I point at the pile.

"Okay and what else?" Beck asks soothingly.

"That's it," I admit sheepishly, my heart rabbiting faster now as I realize how stupid I sound.

"Why don't we do our morning yoga? If you're still feeling overwhelmed after that, I'll look through this paperwork and see what I can help with."

I nod and grab my yoga mat from its spot beside my desk before giving Beck a grateful smile. Beck waves me toward the studio and then heads to the changing room to grab his yoga mat.

I take a moment to take a few breaths and try to get my head on straight.

I roll out my mat and start some stretches to open my chest and help me breathe more easily. By the time Beck saunters back in with his yoga mat, I'm feeling a little more myself.

"Guess who has a date tonight," I brag as Beck stretches into downward dog.

"Hmmm, that's a tough one," Beck mocks.

"Shut up you sarcastic twat," I fire back with a laugh.

"Is this one even halfway worthy of you, love?"

"Time will tell. We've been chatting for a few days, and he seems cool, so I'm crossing my fingers because I need to get laid *so* badly."

"You could always ask Max," Beck suggests, waggling his eyebrows at me.

I huff in frustration at my irritating best friend.

"I told you that you need to drop that. He's *straight*; I don't understand what you don't get about that."

"I don't happen to agree that he's straight," Beck replies with a shrug. "If you ask me, he's at least a little crooked." Beck winks at me, and I can't help but laugh.

"Ah, a boy can dream." I sigh, remembering the weight of Max pinning me down last night, his erection pressing against me. I suppress a shiver. That's nothing but fruitless pining. I'll never have Max, so I need to move on and find a man willing to give me what I need.

Our conversation tapers off as we continue our morning yoga routine. I inhale deeply, letting all my stress and anxiety float away for a few short minutes.

My humiliation over my confession to Max this morning is still niggling at the back of my mind as I work to center my thoughts, focusing only on the movements of my body. I'm glad he was so cool about it, but that was embarrassing as fuck. And when he said he trusts me not to perv on him, I could've melted into a puddle of shame right there in front of him.

"How are you feeling now?" Beck asks once we're finished and rolling up our mats.

"Meh." I shrug. "I'll be okay."

"If there's anything I can do to help, you let me know."

I nod and then retreat to my office again as Beck's class arrives.

My chest still tightens as I look over the never-ending to-do list on my desk. For the love of god, I hope this date works out tonight because I would kill for the physical and mental release that's been just out of my reach for too long. Everything feels like it's piling up, and if I don't find an outlet, I'm going to start bursting at the seams.

Max

The bike I had to fix today turned out to be a bit of a challenge, which I more than welcomed. And by the end of the day, it was running like a dream again.

"I can't thank you enough for fixing it for me. I'm assuming the Triumph out front is yours?" Lynn asks when she picks up her bike in the afternoon.

"She is," I confirm.

"Maybe we could go for a ride together sometime, grab a drink afterward?" she suggests, giving me a smile that's equal parts vixen and girl next door.

I wait for a flare of heat or excitement but come up empty. Even when Lynn bends forward a few inches to flash me a quick peek at her cleavage, nothing stirs in me.

This isn't the first time recently that a beautiful woman has failed to trip my trigger. Maybe it's because it feels so empty? I'm getting tired of just hooking up with strangers. I'd love to connect with someone, to have a relationship. God knows it's been years since I've had the time or energy to give to another person in that way. But, now it feels like time. I'm not a kid anymore; maybe it's time to stop fucking around and get serious about someone.

Lynn jots down her number and passes it across the desk to me.

So, why don't I feel like getting to know her more? She could be a relationship girl, couldn't she? But still, nothing happens.

"Thanks, but I'm not sure that's such a good idea. I have a lot of baggage, you know?" Yes, I'm the douchebag, using my kid as an excuse to let someone down gently.

"Well, if you change your mind."

I nod and put her phone number into my pocket to throw away later when she's not around. Nothing against Lynn, I'm sure she's a sweet girl.

Once she's gone, I get back to work on another car I have waiting, and I do my best to drown out my brothers and get lost in my work.

"Hey bro, your baby mama is here," Gio calls over the whir of my tools.

"Very funny," I call back in a bland tone. I don't know why they both think that's such a funny joke, all fuckin' day long with your *baby mama is here* or *that chick from last weekend just walked in.*

"I'm serious, dude."

I grumble and step around the car to look. I swear I'll strangle him if he's having a laugh at me.

Sure enough, Jess is standing in the lobby, looking put out. She always looks put together, with her red hair styled nicely and her make-up perfect. But today, she looks frazzled somehow.

My gut clenches as I hurry to wipe my hands off and then rush to the front of the shop to see what brought Jess by unexpectedly.

"Is everything okay?" I ask as soon as near her.

"Gigi is fine. Sorry, I didn't mean to worry you. I needed to talk to you, and I didn't want to wait. Can you spare a few minutes?"

"Uh, yeah. You want to grab some lunch down the street?"

Jess nods, and I grab the keys to the shop truck that we use when someone needs a ride somewhere while we work on their car. I don't have to ask where she wants to eat; there's only one place near here that has anything she likes. That was one of the things that irritated the shit out of me when we were dating: how damn picky she was about everything. But we're not dating now, so it's convenient to know without asking where she'll want to go.

We arrive at the trendy little café, and I realize I'm still in my greasy overalls. I step out of the truck and strip my overalls off, leaving me in my street clothes, and toss them in the bed of the truck.

Jess takes in my plain gray t-shirt and worn, holey jeans, and her nose wrinkles. I smirk at her reaction, another one of those things that bugged the hell out of me when we dated, but I couldn't care less about now. I am who I am; she didn't like it and that's okay.

I open the door for her and pull out her chair when we're seated, which seems to appease her after my grungy appearance.

We order and as soon as our waiter is gone, I look at Jess expectantly.

"So, what's so urgent?" I ask.

"I've been seeing someone."

I pause in mid-reach for my glass of water, and I study her expression. That wasn't what I expected her to say, and I can't figure out why she felt she had to rush over to the garage to tell me she has a new boyfriend. Unless she's trying to make me jealous? But that doesn't fit. We've been broken up for *years*, and after her initial shit fit over it she seemed to agree that we weren't a good match.

"Good for you?" I guess at a response.

"He's a great guy," she continues. "He's got an MBA, and he's going to be taking over his father's successful business."

I narrow my eyes. Why is she trying so hard to sell me on this guy?

"Okay."

"He asked me to marry him," she blurts, and everything starts to become a little clearer.

"Oh, that's great." I relax a little. She wants my blessing on a stepfather for Gigi; that makes sense. "I'd love to meet him, if that's okay?"

"Here's the thing, Max." Jess takes a long drink of water then taps her long nails along the glass. "We're moving to New York."

"What?"

"His father's business is expanding and they're opening a new office in New York. It makes sense for him to put Mark in charge out there. So, we're moving to New York...and I'm taking Gigi."

"The hell you are," I roar, slamming my fist down on the table hard enough to rattle our silverware and nearly spill both glasses of water.

Jess glances around and offers apologetic smiles to the people who have suddenly gone quiet and turned their attention in our direction.

"Calm down, Max," Jess hisses.

"I will not calm down." Although, I do make an effort to keep my voice down because shouting isn't going to solve anything. "Over my dead body are you taking my kid from me. I have joint custody, Jess. Like it or not, I have rights and you can't just take Gigi across the damn country."

"If you care about Gigi, you'll see this is the best thing for her. Mark makes enough money that I'll be able to give her a different life. I can enroll her in private school and buy her all the nicest things. Don't you understand that this is what's best for her?"

"What's best for Gigi is to be with her father. I'm going to fight you on this Jess, you can bet on that. I won last time."

"And this time I can afford a much better lawyer," Jess challenges.

Rage burns in my chest, so white hot it threatens to explode. My hands are shaking, and my muscles are tight as I get up from the table and storm out of the restaurant without a backward glance.

I climb into the cab of my truck and slam my fists against the steering wheel, my chest heaving with the effort not to fall apart.

With unsteady hands, I pick up my phone and dial Beck.

"Max, what's up?" Beck answers after a few rings.

"Jess is trying to take Gigi from me, again. I need you to help me, please, I can't lose her." My voice cracks as tears threaten to spill over.

"Okay, take a deep breath. I'm not going to let Jess take Gigi. Why don't we meet this afternoon, and you can tell me exactly what's going on, okay?"

"I still have Gigi tonight. Can we meet to talk about it tomorrow night?"

"Yeah, that works. Don't stress; we'll figure this out."

"Yeah. Thank you so much." I breathe a little easier knowing that Beck will do everything in his power to make sure I get to keep Gigi with me.

But what if it's out of his power? A little voice in the back of my mind nags. What if we have to have one of those bullshit custody agreements where I only get to see Gigi for a month in the summer?

I'm still trembling when I get back to work. Gio and Tony both eye me with concern but are smart enough to keep their distance and not ask too many questions.

CHAPTER 5

Clay

I'm surprised when I get a text from Max midday saying that he doesn't need me to pick Gigi up from school today, that he's got her, and he's taking her out to see a movie and get dinner.

It works just fine for me since I have my date tonight, and now, I have extra time to get ready.

My own classes go by quickly, and when the day ends, I call a quick goodbye to Beck and rush home to get ready.

A nagging feeling has hung around the back of my mind all day long. It's that feeling like I've left the stove on, even though I knew I checked it before I left. But it's not the stove; it's my stupid brain. You'd think knowing that would make it easier to ignore. It doesn't. My heart still races, and my brain still buzzes. It's like having my skull filled with bees. Buzz, buzz, buzz.

I sag against the wall and rub my eyes hard with the heels of my hands, until they start to ache. At least the pain gives my brain something else to focus on.

What if Max and Beck were right and this guy is

a total creep? What if he has a torture dungeon that he's planning to take me to as soon as he has me at his mercy? Ah, right on cue, I missed you my old friend catastrophic thoughts...*not.*

I take a deep breath, hold it for a few seconds, and then slowly let it out. *For the love of god, please let this guy be up for taking care of me tonight.*

I dress in a pair of relaxed fit jeans that hug my ass just right and a gray polo that brings out my steel blue eyes. I take some time styling my hair to messy perfection, and then I step back and assess the finished product.

I look fantastic; now the question will be whether Mr. HotStuff will deserve to unwrap this delectable package.

I jot a quick note for Max telling him I'll— hopefully— be home late, if at all, and then I head out.

When I get to the restaurant, I check my pocket for my wallet three times, then I lock my car door and try the handle three times, and finally I put my keys and cell in my front pocket and...yep, you guessed it, triple checked.

The triple check ritual eases a little tension from my shoulders, enough so that I can move on to the next phase of entering the restaurant.
Inside, it only takes me a second to zero in on the gorgeous, brick shit house of a man waiting at the bar. *Please let that be my date.*

I approach him, and as soon as he notices me, he smiles, his gaze traveling over me with greedy abandon.

"You'd better be the guy I'm meeting, because *damn*," he says.

"I believe I am." I offer my hand to shake. "Clay, nice to meet you."

"Damien, likewise."

When we're led to a table, Damien pulls my chair out for me and doesn't make any suggestions about what I should order, so we're off to a good start.

"What do you like to do for fun?" I ask once we've both decided on what we're ordering.

"I guess I'm kind of a simple guy, give me a cold beer and a football game and I'm happy."

"Do you play any sports?"

"I played football in high school and college. Now, not so much. What about you?"

"I'm a dancer. I own a dance studio, and I dance ballet, hip-hop, and burlesque mainly. And I do yoga."

"Dance and yoga aren't sports," Damien says.

"You're right that yoga is an exercise rather than a sport, but dance is certainly a sport. I entered dance competitions in high school and won trophies; I think that qualifies as a sport," I argue, doing my best to keep my tone pleasant.

Damien snorts, and I clench my hand around my napkin.

"Isn't it a bit *feminine?*"

Lord grant me the strength to not beat this man to death.

"How so?" I ask in a sugary voice. "It's not like any of the dance moves require a vagina."

"You know what I mean; it's not manly."

"I'm sorry, I don't know what you mean."

It could be argued that if I really want to get laid tonight, I should shut up and stop arguing, but this shit bothers the hell out of me. What does this guy have to prove with all his *manly* bullshit? Max is the most masculine dude I've ever met, and he's never turned his nose up at my dancing or anything else.

The waitress chooses that moment to come take our order, and Damien looks visibly relieved to have an out for this conversation.

A year ago, that attitude would've been a deal breaker on the sex front, but beggars can't be choosers. Damien has officially been struck from the *boyfriend material* list, though.

Once our food arrives, we stick to more neutral topics of conversation like the weather and the latest movies we've heard good or bad things about. It's perfectly pleasant and absolutely boring.

While Damien tells me about some dispute he's been having with his neighbor over his neighbor's yappy dog, I wonder to myself if there is a man out there for me after all. Maybe I've been single too long, and now I'm too set in my ways to be in a relationship.

My last serious boyfriend was almost ten years ago when I was in college.

Jake was a great guy. We were assigned to the same dorm freshman year and became instant friends. It only took a few weeks before we were hooking up regularly and not long after that when we decided to be exclusive. We dated all through college, and he's the one who introduced me to Shibari and bondage.

When graduation came, he was offered a job in Philadelphia, and I couldn't bear the idea of leaving Seattle. I didn't want to leave Beck and my mother, and I already had my eye on the perfect location for my dance studio. So, we made the mutual decision to part ways. We still text and Skype a few times a year to catch up and stay in touch.

"What do you think?" Damien asks, and I realize I haven't been listening to a word he's said for the last twenty minutes.

"I think we should pay the bill and go back to your place for dessert."

Damien's apartment is only a few miles away, so I follow him in my car. He offered to leave my car and drive me back to it in the morning, but no way am I planning to stay the night. Not to mention, I'd prefer my own escape route just in case.

"Would you like a drink?" he offers as I toe off my shoes and leave them by the door.

"Sure, I'll take a beer or whatever you've got."

I sit down on the couch and glance around at

the frat boy themed decor. There are several Seattle Seahawk blankets and pillows, a shelf of shot glasses and beer steins, and a plastic basketball hoop attached to one wall.

Damien returns with two beers and plops down on the couch next to me.

"So, I have some ropes and handcuffs, do you have a preference?" he asks conversationally, and my heart starts to pound, and my dick perks up.

"Ropes. I'm, uh, really flexible so you can get creative," I offer before taking a sip of my drink to ease the sudden dryness in my throat. "No pain," I reiterate what I told him over chat before. "No humiliation, either."

"This is going to be fun. The safe word is *potato*, okay?"

I nod and let him take the beer from my hand and place it on the table.

"Come on," he jerks his head toward the back of the apartment, and I follow him down the hall.

"Strip," he commands as soon as we're in his room.

I bristle at the command until I see the ropes lying in the center of his bed. He knows what he's doing; these aren't the rough ropes an amateur would pick up at the hardware store. I shiver in anticipation and grudgingly follow the command.

Once I'm naked, I crawl onto the bed and lay on my stomach.

The bed dips as Damien climbs on. He reaches for the rope and my cock flexes, trapped beneath me, and the pit of my stomach flutters.

It occurs to me that Damien hasn't bothered to try to kiss me or engage in any kind of foreplay, and I'm fine with it. I'm glad we seem to be on the same page with what this is.

He grabs my left arm and roughly yanks it back.

I open my mouth to protest, but when he pulls my left ankle up and starts to bind it to my wrist, I forget what I was going to complain about.

All my thoughts narrow in on the feeling of the rope sliding against my skin and the pleasant tug of my muscles as I settle into the position.

Damien spreads my legs wider and then binds my right arm in the same manner.

My buzzing mind finally settles into the blissful quiet that only comes with being bound and giving my pleasure over to another man.

I'm basking in the glow of the endorphins flooding my brain, when Damien speaks again in a harsh tone.

"You're a filthy slut, aren't you?"

I seethe at his words, all the thrill of being bound and helpless instantly vanishing.

"No, I'm not," I grit out.

His hand comes down bruising on my ass, and I yelp.

"I said no pain," I protest.

"Shut up, slut." He slaps my other ass cheek even harder, and I yowl.

"We're done here," I declare, struggling against the rope binding my hands to my ankles.

"Don't talk back, slut."

Fuck, what was the damn safe word?

"Potato. Potato. Fucking untie me."

Damien let's out an irritated growl but releases me.

"I thought you wanted to play?"

"I told you I don't play like that. Literally, not twenty minutes ago, I said no pain and no humiliation." Damien sits quietly brooding while I hurry to dress and leave without so much as a backward glance. "What the fuck was that? Why didn't you listen when I told you what I needed?"

"I figured it was part of the game. Some guys say they don't get off on that stuff, but they secretly want it."

"You're dumb as hell," I huff. "Here's some free life advice: if someone tells you their limits, fucking listen." And with that, I'm out the door.

Once I'm outside, I let out a groan of frustration. I haven't gotten laid in *ages,* and I'd been so sure Damien was going to give me what I desperately need.

I climb into my car and bang my forehead against the steering wheel. Now I have to go home to my gorgeous, straight roommate once again sexually frustrated.

Maybe I don't really have a crush on Max; maybe my body is just confused because Max is the guy I'm around when I'm blue balling it.

Max

I collapse on the couch after Gigi is in bed.

After my lunch with Jess, I took off from work a little early and picked Gigi up from school. I took her out to her favorite ice cream shop and then we went to see the latest Disney movie. I let her stuff herself with popcorn and called it dinner. I know I'm not winning father of the year on that one, but she had fun, and one night of eating junk food won't kill her.

When we got home, I gave her a bath and read her two stories before she fell asleep.

And somehow, I miss her a little bit now that she's asleep and I'm out here in the living room alone.

I've gotten used to sharing half the week with Jess. But I can't imagine having to wait half a year to see Gigi. More than half the year. She's in school nine months out of the year, so where does that leave me?

I hope to hell there's something Beck can do to help me with this because I can't lose Gigi.

The front door opens, and I crane my neck to see Clay entering.

"I thought you had a date tonight?"

"Ugh, I don't want to talk about it."

I frown and turn to assess him a little more closely. The dude he met up with better not have done something to him, or he's going to have a world of pain coming to him.

"Want to watch something?" I offer.

"Yeah, I'm good with whatever," Clay agrees, plopping down on the couch next to me. "Oh damn, my shitty date made me miss Gigi's bedtime."

My heart stutters. I should tell Clay what happened today with Jess. He's going to be as devastated as I am about the idea of Gigi possibly being taken across the country. But, maybe I can wait until after I talk to Beck about everything. Maybe Beck will tell me this will be easy to fight and then there won't be any reason to upset Clay at all.

I settle back, letting my shoulder bump against Clay's. There's a certain measure of comfort in his presence.

"Do you ever wonder if you're meant to be alone forever?" Clay asks miserably after a few minutes of quietly watching Netflix.

"I don't think about it too much, honestly. I figure if I find the right person, I find the right person, if not, then oh well." I shrug. "Would I like to find someone to spend my life with? Sure. But after being with Jess, I realized that's not something you can force just because you want it."

"Yeah," Clay sighs.

"Hey." I bump my shoulder against his. "You're a catch, any guy would be lucky to have you."

"Why are all the good guys straight?" Clay laments with a pointed look in my direction, and I chuckle.

"Such a tragedy," I agree with a mock serious expression.

"You want me to drop Gigi off at school in the morning?"

"Do you mind? Jess has her for the next few days after this, so you don't have to worry about her in the afternoon. I'll be home late tomorrow, by the way."

"Okay," Clay yawns.

"You look tired, you should get some sleep," I suggest.

"Just a few more minutes," Clay argues, settling his shoulder a little more firmly against mine as if he's craving a little human contact as much as I am.

Clay

Every dish in the kitchen is piled on the table, while I stand on a chair to scrub the insides of the cabinets.

Maybe I can strip and re-stain the wood; that would look nice. Although, I doubt there's any stripper or stain in the house, so I'd have to go to the hardware store. I glance at the clock on the stove. *There probably aren't any hardware stores open at three in the morning.*

Something soft bounces off the back of my head, pulling me from my thoughts. I glance down to see what hit me, and I frown in confusion. I must be more tired than I thought because I can't for the life of me figure out what a random sock is doing lying at my feet.

"What the hell?" I mutter, trying to suppress a yawn.

"I figured you must be a house elf on crack, so I was trying to set you free."

I snort a laugh and glance over my shoulder to see Max standing behind me in nothing but a pair of pajama pants. I force myself not to let my gaze linger on his toned chest or his adorable, sleep rumpled hair.

"Very funny." I roll my eyes and yawn before turning back to continue my task.

Strong hands grasp my waist and, before I know it, I'm being scooped up into Max's arms and carried to my bedroom.

I'm more excited than I have any right to be when Max lowers me onto my bed without so much as jostling me.

"Sleep," he says with authority. I roll my eyes at him.

"I can't sleep; that's why I was cleaning."

He sighs and looks down at me with a conflicted expression.

"What would help?"

A release— something to calm my mind for a few minutes.

"Nothing you can help me with," I toss back with agitation.

"What if I climb into bed with you—"

"Keep talking," I encourage with a salacious grin.

"Dirty mind," Max accuses with a chuckle. "What I was *saying* was, why don't I climb into bed, and we can pull up something boring on your laptop. I bet that'll help you fall asleep."

He's not wrong. It's the only thing that helps some nights. And, truth be told, it's more about the feeling of Max's warmth beside me and the steady rhythm of his breath as he sleeps.

"Thank you."

"Anytime," Max assures me before grabbing my laptop off my desk and climbing into bed beside me.

CHAPTER 6
Max

Waiting all day to meet with Beck was torture. My brothers could tell something was up with me and eased up on some of their bullshit today, so that was a nice reprieve at least.

I was out of the garage at five o'clock on the nose and roaring down the street on my bike to meet with Beck.

My hands are sweaty on my handlebars, and my stomach twists itself in complicated knots all the way to the restaurant where Beck and I had agreed to meet.

I pull into a parking spot around the side of the restaurant and head inside, conscious of the fact that I look like a filthy grease monkey, but also grateful that Beck knows me well enough to know I *am* a good father no matter how messy I may look after a day of work.

"Max," Beck calls out from a table to the left of the host's station. He stands and offers his hand when I approach the table.

Beck is dressed in a pink blouse and black skinny jeans and has pink high heels on. His face has light make-up today, and I notice there's a certain lightness to his expression that wasn't there before he met Gage.

"Thanks for meeting with me. You know, being in love looks good on you."

"Aw, thanks you big sap."

I chuckle. He's not wrong.

I take a seat, and a waitress appears to take our drink orders. We make small talk for a few minutes about how Beck is liking life after corporate law and what it's like living with Gage.

"Nox has been trying to talk me into letting him give me a tattoo, but after the peacock Gage did, I'm not eager for any more needles," Beck explains. Nox is the boyfriend of Gage's best friend. I've met the whole Heathens Ink crew on a few occasions when Beck has invited Clay and me out to the bar; they all seem like good guys.

"What's he want to ink on you?" I ask.

"Well, he does these mythical creatures that are pretty badass. He did a griffin for Adam, a unicorn on Madden, and a Siren on Dani. He's going to give Gage a dragon to symbolize strength, and he said he wants to do a pixie for me because pixies are full of light and laughter."

"That sounds perfect for you," I agree.

We lapse into silence for a few seconds before I decide to bite the bullet and get into the reason we're here.

"Jess told me yesterday that she's engaged and planning to move to New York. Obviously, she wants to take Gigi with her. But I can't let that happen. I can't stand the thought of only seeing her for a month or two in the summer and missing her the rest of the year."

Beck frowns and rubs his chin.

"That's going to be tricky. If I remember correctly, you agreed that disputes would be settled in mediation. If you can't work it out and it goes to arbitration, they're likely going to side with the mother. With Gigi being school age, they're not going to split the school year. You may be able to get winter break as well as summer, maybe spring break, but..." Beck trails off and shakes his head, and my stomach plummets.

"So, what do I do?" I ask desperately.

"Let me think this over, and let's set up mediation to see if the two of you can reach any sort of agreement," he suggests, but I can still hear the *but* hanging in the air. This is hopeless. Jess is going to take Gigi all the way across the country, and I'll only get to see her a few times a year.

I know I'm an asshole through our meal, unable to summon the common courtesy to hold a proper conversation while my heart breaks over the thought of losing Gigi, and my blood boils at Jess doing this to me. I should find whoever this douchebag fiancé is and punch him in the nose.

I flick on the light in the garage and take a deep breath, letting the scent of motor oil and grease calm me.

I grew up working in the garage. It's no surprise that the scent smells like home to me.

I run my hand over the frame of '67 Norton Commando I'm restoring.

Some people might think it's weird that I would want to work on cars all day and then come home and do more work. But restoring classic bikes isn't work for me. It's been my passion since I was sixteen, and I got my first bike at a junkyard and rebuilt it from the ground up. There's no thrill like taking something that's broken and rusted and making it beautiful again.

"Hey, I thought you might be out here," Clay says, peeking his head out of the door.

"Yeah, what's up?"

"Oh nothing, just wanted to say hi and see how your day was."

Clay's interest in my daily life never fails to warm me inside.

"Kinda sucked," I admit. "Let me work for a little bit, and then I'll come in and tell you about it over a few drinks?"

"Sounds good," he agrees with a smirk.

I'm not sure how long I spend outside working, but when I go inside Clay is lying on the couch watching *Will & Grace* and I hesitate in the entrance to the living room. I know I have to tell him about Jess, but I really need a fucking drink first.

"Hey, sweetie. You okay?"

"Yeah," I answer with an uncharacteristic gruffness to my voice. "I need a drink, and then I have to tell you something. You want a drink?"

"Sure." Clay sits up, worry clouding his eyes.

For some reason, I notice that he looks kind of cute with his hair all mussed from lying down.

I shake off the odd thoughts and head toward the kitchen to get the bottle of Jack I keep above the fridge.

"You're worrying me; did something happen?" Clay asks, appearing in the kitchen doorway.

I unscrew the cap on the bottle and take a drink before waving Clay back to the living room.

"Jess stopped by to talk yesterday."

"Is something wrong with Gigi?" Clay gasps.

"No, but Jess is engaged, and they're planning to move to New York in six months," I reveal, and when Clay doesn't react, I continue. "She says she's taking Gigi."

"What? She can't do that! Can she?"

"Beck didn't seem too confident, honestly. The Parenting Plan we agreed to says that in a dispute like this we have to deal with it in mediation, and if we can't reach an agreement, then it goes to arbitration."

"What happens at arbitration?"

"Jess and I would present our sides of the case in front of a small panel, and they'd get to decide who Gigi goes with."

Clay looks as devastated as I feel and, for that, I swear I could kiss him.

"We can't let Jess take her."

"We'll keep thinking, and in the meantime,

we'll drink." I salute him with the bottle and take another gulp before passing it to him. He hesitates for a second before taking it and drinking as well.

The hours pass, and the whiskey slowly disappears between the two of us.

Clay repeats a joke he heard, and I collapse against his side in a laughing fit.

"Sorry," I apologize when he tenses under my touch.

"Don't be, this is the most action I've gotten in ages."

"See, that's something I just don't get. How are you single? You're a gorgeous, successful business owner. And don't think I haven't seen how flexible you are when you're doing yoga in the living room."

Clay's pouty lips morph into a sly smile, his eyelids drooping slightly from the alcohol he's consumed.

"If you're trying to get into my pants, flattery will get you everywhere," Clay slurs and then giggles.

An unexpected rush of heat licks at my skin.

"Seriously, though," I prompt.

Clay's smile fades a bit, and he's suddenly very interested in taking another drink. I wait patiently, my curiosity overwhelming.

"Are you sure you want to know this? It's a sex thing," he warns, his cheeks—already pink from the liquor—tinge even darker.

"Now I'm even more interested to know. Do you have an extra dick or something?"

My eyes dart over Clay, trying to imagine what could be wrong with his body physically. I've seen just about every inch of him, as tends to happen when you're roommates.

Clay laughs before meeting my eyes cautiously. "God, this is embarrassing. I have a kink."

I'm too drunk to manage any kind of poker face, and I'm sure my raised eyebrows and shocked smirk say it all.

"Do tell," I prompt, leaning forward unconsciously. What kind of kink could my meticulous, responsible roommate be so into that it affects his ability to have a relationship? "Oh wait, can I try to guess?"

Clay snorts and takes another drink before passing me the bottle. He brandishes his hand in a gesture to tell me to go right ahead.

"Okay, let me think. It must be something really freaky if it scares guys away," I stroke my chin, and Clay crosses his arms, regarding me with challenge. "Oh, is it the thing where you want a dude to change your diaper and like feed you a bottle?"

Clay's mouth drops open, and he lets out a barking laugh. "No, definitely not."

"Oh, I know; you want to be a puppy," I guess again.

"No." Clay shakes his head again. "Where are you even coming up with this stuff?"

"*Real Sex* on HBO."

"You're not even close."

I lean back and let my gaze wander over Clay again, trying to picture what a man like him might really be into in bed. Maybe it's not as out there as I'm thinking; maybe it's just something he's embarrassed about.

"I've got it; you're totally into being dominated."

Clay's easy smile turns tense, and his eyes dart away from me.

"No, I *don't* like to be dominated." His voice is rough, and I can tell that I must've hit somewhere close to the mark or at least struck a nerve.

"You don't have to tell me if it's too uncomfortable for you, but I hope you know it doesn't make a damn bit of difference to me what you're into in bed. You can be a furry for all I care."

Clay relaxes a little and chuckles again. He still doesn't meet my eyes as he fiddles with a throw blanket over the back of the couch and shifts around like he's trying to find a more comfortable way to sit.

"I'm...uh...really into bondage," he finally admits.

A strange spike of heat goes through me at the confession.

"Oh?" My voice comes out sounding like gravel as my mind conjures up images of Clay with his wrists bound by a length of rope. "I'm surprised the guys you're trying to date aren't into that. Or at the very least can't be persuaded to give it a try."

"Yeah, the bondage itself isn't the issue. The issue is most guys who are into bondage are into dominance and submission, which I'm definitely *not* into," Clay explains. "Plus, it's a big trust thing, so picking up a stranger to tie me up isn't exactly ideal."

A protective surge pulses through me in equal measure to the surprising lust this conversation has evoked. My skin feels hot and tight, like I might explode out of it at the wrong move. The idea of a man being rough or punishing to Clay when that isn't what he wants makes me want to break something. Even worse is the thought of Clay feeling helpless or nervous with someone he doesn't know or trust.

My fists clench, and my heart thunders.

Without thought, I reach for Clay, my fingers grazing the soft skin on his forearm, imagining what he would look like completely at my mercy.

I shift in my seat, and the minor friction of my pants against my achingly hard cock is almost enough for me to lose it. I've never been this turned on in my life, and my alcohol soaked brain doesn't give a shit that it's a guy I'm imagining pinned beneath me.

"This conversation is making you uncomfortable," Clay notes apologetically.

Yes, but not in the way you would think.

"No, I'm just drunk."

Clay sets the nearly empty bottle of Jack aside and gets to his feet as gracefully as a newborn giraffe.

"Come on, love, let's go to bed." I know Clay doesn't mean it *that* way, but his words are husky and oddly inviting as they roll around in my alcohol sodden brain.

CHAPTER 7

Clay

I wake up with the taste of stale whiskey in my mouth and a feeling of dread in the pit of my stomach.

I groan and press the palms of my hands against my eyes.

I can't believe I told Max about my kink last night. He must think I'm a total freak now. He's probably disgusted by me or laughing behind my back. Fuck, I hate myself so much. Max is going to kick me out and never talk to me again. Then he's going to tell everyone what a freak I am.

I grab my phone to check the time and notice a missed text from Beck.

> **Beck:** I'm running late this morning, so I won't have time for morning yoga before my classes.
> **Clay:** You're running behind? Color me shocked lol
> **Beck:** *gives you the middle finger* It's not my fault; SOMEONE woke up and begged for morning sex
> **Clay:** That someone was you, wasn't it?
> **Beck:** Totally ;) but it's not my fault that Gage

is the sexiest, most perfect man alive, and I want to spend every second wrapped around him.

Clay: TMI dude. Have a good morning; see you in a few hours.

I stretch and groan again. This is one of the main reasons I rarely drink; my poor dehydrated muscles get way too tight. And if Beck is blowing me off for morning yoga, that means I can do it in the peace of my living room instead of at the studio.

I roll out of bed and tug on a pair of yoga pants and a red V-neck t-shirt and then I run my fingers through my hair. I grab my yoga mat from my closet, my iPod from my dresser, and then I head into the living room.

I roll out my mat and pop in my earbuds. I start with Downward Dog to get a good stretch of my back and arms. I wish like hell I was sore from being tied up.

My stomach clenches at the thought, and heat rolls through my body.

I shake off the images because doing yoga with an erection isn't ideal. Then I move into my next pose, this one a little more complicated and better to loosen my stiff muscles.

Max

I wake up feeling strangely off balance. It may be the hangover, or possibly the shit going down with Jess, but something else is nagging in the back of my mind. It's like a dream you can't quite remember after you wake up.

I reach under the covers and lazily cup my epic morning erection. *It must've been a damn hot dream I can't remember.*

Images of smooth flesh dance behind my eyelids. It's been way too long since I've had a woman in my bed; that's the problem.

So why did I turn down the babe with the motorcycle the other day? It doesn't make any sense how I can be this damn horny and fail to get excited by a beautiful woman giving me her number.

Maybe I need to stop being so hung up on instant sparks and just try to get back on the horse.

My alarm starts sounding from my phone, so I pull my hand off my dick and roll out of bed with a groan. I'm too groggy to be bothered with throwing on anything other than a pair of boxers to head to the kitchen to start coffee before I take a shower. Clay isn't usually up by now anyway, and even if he is, I don't care about him seeing me nearly naked.

I stumble out of my bedroom and head for the kitchen. But when I cut through the living room, I stop dead in my tracks: my stomach bottoms out, and my heart jumps into my throat.

Clay is on his stomach with his hands wrapped around both ankles, stretching his legs to touch his head.

And that's when I remember the conversation we had last night about Clay being into bondage.

"Max, please," An echo of Clay's pleas in my dream sounds in my mind and nearly knocks me on my ass.

I stand there mesmerized as Clay releases his ankles and lays flat for a few seconds, just watching his back rise and fall with each measured breath.

Of their own volition, my eyes roam over the hard lines of Clay's frame, and then for a just a second over his round ass. I can almost imagine what those taut globes would feel like under my hands.

What the fuck is wrong with me?

I draw in a sharp breath and whip around to flee the room before Clay can notice me standing there, watching him with a tent in the front of my boxers.

I sprint to the kitchen, my chest heaving and my mind spinning like tires stuck in the mud.

I did *not* just get a boner for Clay, *right?* It's not possible. I'm *straight.* I've always been straight.

I don't have anything against gay dudes; hell, Clay is my favorite person on the damn planet save for Gigi. But I like women. I like their soft curves and sweet smell. I like smooth skin and long, fruity scented hair. I am *straight.*

My hands are shaking as I set about making coffee. Something routine and soothing that grounds me in who I am and what my life is.

Clay is my best friend, my bro. You don't just wake up one day at the age of thirty-two and suddenly want to bone your bro.

I had a weird dream, and I'm hungover; that's all. And the idea of bondage is hot. That has nothing to do with Clay; he's just the one who happened to mention it to me, and now my brain is equating the two.

"Oh hey, I didn't hear you get up. Are you feeling as rough as I am this morning?" Clay asks, coming into the kitchen behind me.

I startle and nearly spill the water as I pour it into the coffee maker.

"Yeah, real rough," I agree in a gruff voice, my pulse pounding loudly in my ears.

"You okay?" Clay asks, likely noticing the way my hands tremble as I press the button to start coffee.

"Fine. I'm going to jump in the shower." I force a smile and slip past Clay, trying not to notice the confused and worried look in his expressive brown eyes.

In the bathroom, I crank the knob on the shower to the hottest setting and strip out of my clothes, leaving them piled on the floor.

I step under the scalding stream and close my eyes to picture a motorcycle engine, and then I mentally take it apart and rebuild it in my mind until I start to feel myself centered and even again.

I'm still the guy who loves motorcycles and his daughter. I'm still the guy who enjoys women but was never much of a skirt chaser. I'm still the guy with a best friend I can count on in all things. *I'm still me.*

I rinse the soap off my body, refusing to linger on my still semi-erect cock, and then I shut off the water and reach for a towel.

See? A shower was all I needed to feel like myself again. My brain was a little scrambled this morning, no big deal.

With a towel secure around my waist, I step out of the bathroom cautiously, listening for Clay.

The house seems to be silent, and I let out the breath I was holding and hustle down the hall to my room.

I toss my towel onto the bed and quickly grab a pair of boxers and jeans from my dresser and tug them on before my dick can get any more crazy ideas.

After I tug a shirt over my head and run my fingers through my damp hair, I realize that I was a complete dick to Clay this morning. He was nervous to tell me about his kink last night, and this morning, I probably gave him the impression that I'm freaked out about it.

I shove my phone into my pocket and head down the hall toward Clay's room to see if he's still home, so I can apologize.

I find his door open and his room empty, and my shoulders sag. I'll have to make it up to him tonight and assure him that no matter what he gets off on, it's not going to change our friendship.

I turn to leave when something in his open closet catches my eye.

I know I shouldn't. I know it's an invasion of privacy. But I can't stop my feet from carrying me the few feet closer to get a better look.

After what he told me last night, it's no surprise to find several black ropes hanging beside his clothes. But for some reason, the sight makes my breath catch and my cock thicken against my thigh.

With a trembling hand, I reach out and run a single finger over the length of the rope. So soft to the touch. I take one in my hand and wrap it briefly around my fist, and something deep inside me clicks into place.

My cock is hard and throbbing in the confines of my jeans now as images flash through my mind of a petite body bound and laid out just for me to play with and bring pleasure to.

I drop the rope and try to shake it off.

Out of the corner of my eye, I notice something lying on the floor just inside the closet. It looks like a photograph. I know I shouldn't look. I don't want to invade his privacy. But, my curiosity gets the better of me, and I find myself reaching for the item.

My fingers glide over the smooth surface of the picture, and as I take in the image, my hands start to tremble.

The picture is of Clay. He looks like he's about ten years younger here, his hair a bit longer, and his limbs a little more gangly with less muscle. But Clay's adorable youth isn't the most notable thing about this picture. *That* element is the same black rope that I just had in my hands. It's woven around Clay's arms, binding them together. I trace my finger around the outline of the image, my breath huffing out between my lips. My eyes travel away from his bound hands to Clay's face. My gut twists with an ache of confusing longing as I take in the look of pure ecstasy coloring his features.

I should put the photo back on the floor and walk away. *But I can't.*

Holding the picture against my chest, I hurry to my room, open the top drawer of my dresser, and shove it inside before I can let my better judgment talk me out of it.

My entire body is strung tight and pulsing with need. Ten minutes before work isn't the time to be contemplating new kinks. I let out a slow breath and rub my hands over my face. I need to get a grip. I have to get to work, and I can't go in there with a raging hard-on.

My legs carry me to the bathroom where I turn on the cold water in the sink and then splash some on my face. *I have to get a grip.*

Clay

I pace outside of Studio One, counting the minutes until Beck's class lets out.

Max is going to kick me out. I'm going to end up homeless. I'll have to live in my car. I'll never see Gigi again. Of course, I won't see Gigi again; Max won't let a perverted freak like me around his kid.

"Hey, whoa, take a deep breath." I hear Beck's voice from behind me, and I realize I'm clutching the wall and dragging in shallow breaths.

I close my eyes and force myself to pull in a deep breath, holding it in my lungs for a three count before slowly letting it out.

"Let's go to your office," Beck suggests after I manage a few more breaths.

"But...your class," I argue.

"It's over, sweetie. Come on."

I let Beck lead me to my office and guide me to my chair. I feel like such an idiot when I see the concern in his expression.

"I'm fine, just catastrophic thoughts and all that fun stuff. I'll be okay," I assure him in spite of the fact that my hands are still shaking, and my heart is still jumping in my chest like a frog on crack.

"What happened?"

"Max is going to kick me out, and I'm going to be homeless."

"What? Why would Max kick you out?" Beck asks. "Oh, is he going to move to New York instead of trying to fight for custody?"

"What? No. Wait, do you think he's going to move to New York?" I gasp, my gut tightening. "Oh my god, he's going to move to New York, and then

I'll never see him *or* Gigi ever again, and I'll still be homeless."

"Babe, you *need* to calm down," Beck insists. "I was just taking a guess. I doubt Max will move to New York; his job and family are here. Now, why do you think you'll be homeless?"

"Max and I were drinking last night, and I..."

"Oh my god, you totally kissed him," Beck gasps with glee.

"No! Holy hell, what is wrong with you?"

"What's wrong with me? How the hell are you living with a man like that and not trying to jump him every second?"

"Because he's *straight*," I point out for the umpteenth time.

"If you didn't try to kiss him, what happened?"

"I told him about the bondage stuff."

"Was he mean to you about it? Because I will march right over there and shove my foot up his ass if he made you feel bad about something he has no business even having an opinion on."

"He wasn't mean, but I can tell it freaked him out. He seemed okay at first, but then he got really quiet, and this morning he couldn't get away from me fast enough."

"Oh sweetie," Beck comes around my desk and crouches beside my chair, placing a comforting hand on my knee. "If he doesn't accept you for who you are, then fuck him."

I snort and bury my face in my arms on my

desk. "It's not that easy, and you know it. He's my best friend."

"Hey," Beck protests and a laugh manages to escape from my tight chest.

"My *other* best friend," I correct. "I care about him, and I don't want to lose him over this."

"I know." Beck rubs my leg and rests his forehead against my shoulder. "If Max is really your best friend, he'll come around. Maybe he is weirded out, but I'm sure he'll get over it. He's a good guy; you know that."

I swallow hard and nod even though I'm not entirely convinced.

"Shit, I've got to pull myself together before my class gets here," I lament, sitting up and smoothing my shirt.

"Do you need me to take it for you today?"

"No. Thank you, but it'll help me get my mind off everything."

"Okay, well if you need anything, you let me know. And if you need me to kick Max in the balls, you know I'll do that, too."

"You're his lawyer; isn't that against some sort of ethics code?" I laugh.

"Fine, I'll get Gage to kick him in the balls."

"Thanks, boo." I give Beck a quick kiss on the cheek and then head to the studio, so I can try to center myself before my class arrives.

CHAPTER 8

Max

No matter how hard I try, I can't shake the memory of the silk rope in my palm. I figured work would take my mind off it, but my fixation has only grown stronger as the day progressed.

All I can think about is getting home to find out more from Clay and do some internet research of my own.

"Guess who I ran into at the bar last night," Gio says, bumping his shoulder against mine as I work a tire off an old Chevy.

"No idea, Gio. And you know I hate guessing games."

My brother rolls his eyes at my lack of enthusiasm for his little game.

"It was Nina."

"My ex from like ten years ago?"

"Yeah and she was still fine as hell. I thought for sure you would wife her up."

I bristle and clench my jaw, forcing my attention to remain on the tire I'm in the middle of replacing.

Nina was my high school sweetheart, and she was a great girl. I was well aware that my entire family and hers expected I'd put a ring on it after graduation. It didn't matter that we were clearly too young and had no fucking clue which way was up. Hell, at thirty-two I still feel too young for something as serious as marriage most days. But, more than that, there was just something *missing*. I loved Nina, but there was no passion, no excitement.

"Just didn't fit, bro," I tell him with a shrug. "I don't go around asking you why you haven't married every girl you've taken to bed."

Gio laughs and slaps me on the shoulder.

"Good point. I just hate thinking of you lonely, man. You know, you could always move in with me and Tony; we've still got one more extra bedroom."

Live with both my brothers? Fucking shoot me now.

"No thanks, Gio." I can barely stand to spend ten minutes at their place with the dirty sock and piss smell. It's like they live in a damn frat house and neither of them is willing to pick up after themselves. They're goddamn animals.

"It's just Tony and I have been thinking that maybe living with that que—"

The impact gun whirs in my hands as I tighten the lug nuts, cutting off the abhorrent slur my brother just dropped like it was nothing. I spin on him and fix him with a warning look.

"I told you not to call him that. While you're at it, erase that fucking word from your vocabulary, asshole."

Gio holds his hands up in surrender.

"I didn't mean it like that. Just that he's a fa —uh...he's *feminine*."

"Oh yeah, how so?" I challenge. Gio takes a step back and casts around, likely looking for backup. He knows better than to get into this with me. After he and Tony met Clay for the first time, they certainly had something to say, and I laid down the law.

"Okay, listen...all I'm saying is we figured maybe living with him is starting to rub off and that's why you haven't been dating lately."

"Jesus, you two are morons," I mutter, turning back to my current task.

"It's true though. When was your last date?"

I pause while I try to recall. And, sadly, it takes me way too long to come up with an answer. "Maybe eight months." It's been over a year, but if I tell him that, this conversation will never end.

"*Dude*," Gio gasps. "Is your dick broken or something?"

"My dick is fine," I grit through my teeth. Jesus, will this conversation ever end? My dick is in perfect working order; I had an epic hard on just this morning...after a dream about Clay.

I shake that thought off because it's not helping anything. I already determined this morning that I'm as straight as I've ever been. A few errant thoughts after a year of celibacy are almost expected. Gio is dead wrong about Clay having anything to do with my dry spell, but maybe he has a point about me going out and getting laid.

"Fine, just wanted you to know we worry about you."

"I'm glad to know you two spend so much time thinking about my dick," I quip.

"Hey, fuck you," Gio retorts with a chuckle. And then he *finally* walks away and lets me get back to my damn work.

But even once he walks away, his words nag at me. Could I use a warm body in my bed? Hell yeah. Do I have time to date or even go pick someone up? Not even close. Between Gigi, work, and restoring vintage bikes on the side, I don't have time for any of that shit. And now with everything Jess is putting me through, the last thing I need to be worried about is getting my dick wet.

I'll find time to have fun once everything falls into place. But that doesn't mean I don't still want to do some personal research on all that bondage stuff. Maybe it'll come in handy when I am able to enjoy a little playtime.

Clay

I stand at the front door with my hands shaking, too afraid to open the door and face Max's disgust. I shouldn't have said anything to him last night. I've ruined everything, and there's no way to go back and fix it now.

Okay, on the count of three I'll go in. One...two...two and a half...

The door opens, and Max smiles at me with confusion.

"I thought I heard someone out here. Why are you standing here instead of coming inside?"

"Uh…" I shove my hands in my pockets and try to think of a plausible excuse aside from *I was afraid to face you*. My mind buzzes with the white noise that makes it impossible to think straight, and Max is still staring at me, waiting for me to say something. "I feel like I'm failing at everything. I feel like my life is falling apart in my hands," I blurt.

"What? No, it's not," Max tries to reassure me.

"I know, but that's how it *feels*. I'm treading water and getting farther in over my head every day. It's all too much. And now you're creeped out by me and want me to move out."

"Where'd you get that idea? I'm sorry I don't know what to say when you get like this. Please, come inside."

I huff out a laugh and look up at Max through my moist eyelashes.

"Trust me, as helpless as it feels from your end, it feels a thousand times worse inside my head. With the catastrophic thoughts, it's like I *want* you to agree with me that the worst is about to happen because it'll validate me. But at the same time, I don't want you to agree because that means all my worst fears are coming true."

"How about if I just give you a hug?" Max offers helplessly, opening his arms to me.

I nod with a small smile on my lips and step

into his arms. "I don't know what I'd do without you," I mumble against his chest.

"Ah, you'd be fine. Now, get in here; I made dinner."

"You did?" I ask in surprise.

"Well, it was a frozen pizza. But I didn't burn it, so I think I still deserve the credit."

I chuckle. "Of course, you deserve credit. Thanks for cooking."

I follow Max to the kitchen; when he reaches into the fridge, he holds up a beer questioningly.

"No thanks, I'm still feeling the effects of last night. Just my liver's way of reminding me I'm not twenty-two anymore."

"Right? God, I'm glad I'm not the only one feeling every one of my thirty-two years today."

I nod in agreement and accept the soda he hands me instead. A little knot of tension eases in my chest. Everything feels normal. This is totally fine; he just needed a minute to adjust to it.

"Can I ask you a few questions about the bondage thing?" Max asks, and I accidentally inhale while taking a sip of my soda.

I set the can down and start to cough and sputter against the fizzy liquid now burning down my trachea instead of my esophagus.

Max reaches over and thumps his large hand against my back until I stop coughing.

"What...uh...what kinds of questions?" I ask once I catch my breath again.

Max doesn't answer right away, and I feel my face

heating as I keep my gaze trained on a slice of pepperoni on my piece of pizza.

"How did you know that was what you were into?" he finally asks.

I shrug as I pick off the pepperoni and shove it in my mouth. "I had a boyfriend who was into it," I answer after thoroughly chewing.

"That's not all there is to it. If that was it, you wouldn't be having trouble dating."

I sigh and finally look up at Max, whose expression is full of open curiosity. "Okay, you know I have anxiety? Well, it's always been bad when it comes to sex. I don't really know why, I just could never turn my brain off and relax enough to *really* enjoy it. Then, I dated this guy in college who was into bondage, and that was pretty much it. I was able to go to this really Zen place in my head and just *feel*. It's kind of like a drug, though. Now sex without bondage doesn't really do it for me in the same way. I still cum, but it's not as intense. I'm too in my own head."

My pulse thunders in my ears as I wait for Max's reaction. I've never even given a full explanation to Beck.

Max nods thoughtfully but doesn't say anything for two hundred heartbeats. "So, you didn't really know until you tried it?"

"I guess, yeah." I take another big bite and pray for this conversation to find a quick conclusion. I don't understand why Max wants to know all this anyway.

"Huh. I was thinking it seems kind of...interesting."

"Interesting?"

Max shifts in his seat, and now, it seems to be his turn to avoid my gaze. "Yeah, I don't know. Theoretically, where would someone find out more about how it works and everything?"

"The internet?"

"Duh," Max laughs. "But I don't just want porn. Do you know of any instructional type videos?"

"Google Shibari, there's some porn, but lots of helpful stuff, too," I answer with a dry throat. Is Max really into the idea of bondage? As if there needs to be one more way he's perfect and still completely straight.

"Oh okay, I'll do that then."

Something flashes through Max's eyes that I can almost imagine is disappointment. But it can't be. It's not like he wanted me to offer to teach him. I wouldn't be able how to teach him how to bind anyway, all I know is how to relax and enjoy being bound.

Heat flares at the base of my spine just imagining Max straddling my chest as his rough fingers wind my soft ropes around my wrists and attach them to my headboard.

"Did you talk to Jess yet about mediation?" I ask, desperate to change the subject.

"Not yet, I'm going to talk to her when I pick up Gigi this weekend. I figure giving it a few days to settle is a good idea. The last thing I need is to say or do something that she can use against me."

"Good thinking," I agree.

After we finish eating, I clean up our plates while Max takes out the garbage. It really is too bad he's straight because we'd make a great couple. But it's useless to long for things that will never be.

Normally, Max and I hang out after dinner, but tonight I'm feeling a little too raw from my high anxiety day and the new development of Max apparently being into bondage—just not with me. I decide to slip into my room to get some space from him tonight.

I close my door behind me and flop down on my bed just as my Skype ringtone sounds on my phone. There's only one person I Skype with.

I glance in my mirror quickly to make sure I look presentable and then hit the accept call button.

"Hey Jake," I greet my smiling ex-boyfriend when his face fills my screen.

"Hey, babe. How's it going?"

"Ugh," is the only response I can come up with that isn't a lie.

Jake chuckles and the sound warms me. He's always had a nice laugh.

"Uh-oh, what's wrong?"

"Nothing, just life. My sex life is non-existent, my gorgeous roommate might be into bondage but is still straight as an arrow, and all the stress of running a business is hell on my complexion."

"Sugar, it sounds to me like the answer to all of

your problems is the same thing. You need someone to take care of you. You're wound too tightly, and you need to be unraveled." Jake's voice takes on a husky quality he always used when he was sweet talking me into bed. Not that he ever had to put that much effort into it.

"Stop it with that charming shit; you know it doesn't work on me anymore."

Jake sighs and then chuckles. "Pity. I didn't mean me, though. I only meant that I remember how much good a proper release always did for you."

"Yeah, I almost can't remember what that feels like. Do you have this much trouble finding partners?"

"I don't *need* the ropes like you do, love," Jake Points out and a wave of self-pity washes over me.

Why do I have to be so broken that it's impossible for me to find someone? Maybe I should forget the bondage altogether and settle for a lackluster sex life with someone I could build a life with. My chest aches both in longing and disappointment at the idea. Why can't I have both? Is it so much to ask to want a life partner as well as someone willing to tie me up and use my body until I'm spent and boneless?

"Yeah," I sigh. "I'm probably going to be alone forever."

"No, you aren't. You're a catch; I still regret ever letting you get away."

I roll my eyes at my friend. "I told you that shit isn't going to work."

"I know, but you can't blame a guy for trying. Tell me something good going on in your life."

I settle back against my pillow and tell Jake all about On Pointe and about my wonderful friends and the LGBTQ youth center—Rainbow House—that I've been volunteering at.

"You've got a good life, Clay. As much as I miss you sometimes, I'm glad you stayed where your happiness is."

"Thanks, Jake. It's getting late, and I had a long day, so I think I'm going to get some sleep." We sign off, and I strip out of my clothes, leaving them in a pile beside my bed. And then I snuggle under my blankets and drift off to sleep, doing everything in my power *not* to wonder if Max is enjoying his Google exploration of bondage.

CHAPTER 9

Max

When I get back inside from taking out the trash, Clay is closed in his room. My gut tightens as I wonder if I pushed too hard, asked too much. I could tell Clay was uncomfortable discussing it. But I can't shake my fascination.

My body aches from unloading the shipment of tires we got in today. I'd kill for a back massage and a hot bath. But I'm too tired to get back up once I've collapsed on my bed.

I wiggle out of my pants and toss them on the floor. My shirt joins them a second later, and I sigh at the blissful feeling of my cool sheets against my heated skin. My cock lays half hard against my thigh, beckoning me to tug out a relaxing release before I fall asleep. I spent the day getting hard every time my mind wandered, and now my balls are heavy and sore.

I suddenly remember the picture of Clay I found this morning, and my cock is back to full mast within seconds.

I groan quietly as I try to fight the urge to pull the picture out and study it again. It would be *so* wrong.

I wrap my hand around my thick length and give it a slow stroke from root to tip. My eyes fall closed and my brain immediately conjures the image of Clay bound and steeped in pleasure. I gasp and bite down on my bottom lip.

My balls jostle and ache as I jerk myself faster. My chest heaves with heavy, panting breaths.

I can almost hear the way Clay might gasp and plead when he's bound and being worked to the edge. I can imagine the way his smooth skin would feel under my rough fingers as I'd tease and pleasure him until we're both pulsing and desperate for release.

My cock stiffens in my hand, and I whimper. My free hand plays over my sensitive nipples and down my stomach as I thrust harder into my fist.

I imagine Clay's eyes shining with lust, his full lips falling open, and his head tilting back as he gasps my name.

My release barrels through me, spurting over my stomach, and I stroke myself through it.

I'm trembling from the intensity of my orgasm as I reach for my dirty t-shirt to mop my cooling cum off my stomach. Then, I toss it back on the floor and let the shame and confusion wash over me.

I feel like I don't even know myself anymore. And the key to all this seems to be bondage.

I grab my laptop and prop myself up against my pillow. I start my search sticking to articles and info pages like Wikipedia to get a basic understanding of bondage and specifically about the kind of bondage Clay mentioned—Shibari. Apparently, Shibari is Japanese bondage art, and it's absolutely spectacular. It's sensual and visually stunning. I can't get enough of it as I scan through image after image.

I'm enamored with the beauty of it, but it's not exactly getting my dick hard. I decide to go all in and click on one of the porn videos.

I pop in my ear buds so Clay won't overhear—although I'm sure he already assumes I'm looking at bondage stuff since I did just ask him about it.

It's not until the video starts that I realize it's guy on guy. I almost click away out of reflex, but then I decide to give it a minute *just to see.*

The smaller of the two men efficiently strips out of his clothes with little finesse. It's clear he's eager to get to the bondage part of the video by the way he hurries to present himself to the other man. A little electric thrill runs up my spine as the small man turns his back to the camera and grabs his elbows.

The camera zooms in to focus on his arms and back as the larger hands start to thread the colorful rope through his arms, around his torso, and back again. It doesn't take long for a beautiful design to emerge.

Then, the bound man is lead to a chair, and I notice his chest is already heaving, and his cock is hard. Not just hard, throbbing red, and leaking pre-cum. He's painfully aroused from being tied, without a single other touch so far.

The larger man continues to work, now binding the small man to the chair. Every time the rope brushes his skin, his cock heaves and a whimper falls from his lips.

It's easy to picture Clay in that role—wanting, *needing*, desperate for me—aching and gasping for me to take care of him.

My own hot longing settles in the pit of my stomach, my cock resting hard again against my stomach.

What the fuck is wrong with me?

I whip the ear buds out and slam my laptop shut.

Desperately, I close my eyes and try to picture the beautiful woman from the shop the other day—Lynn—bound and begging for me. The image is appealing, but it doesn't hold the same heat the thought of Clay did, and I don't know what the fuck to do with that.

I'm straight. I've always been straight. You don't go thirty-two years only ever looking at women, and then one day want to tie up and fuck a man.

I wish there was someone I could talk to about this. Someone who could assure me that I'm not going crazy. Maybe this is a phase; maybe it's just Clay's kink that has me going. Right now, there are too many *what ifs* and *maybes* to risk my friendship with Clay.

CHAPTER 10

Clay

"Hey love, how are you feeling this morning?" Beck asks as soon as I walk into On Pointe the next morning.

"Mostly better."

"Uh-huh, go on," Beck prompts.

"Max was cool about the bondage stuff...too cool, actually."

"What do you mean?"

"He was, like, *into* it, I think," I divulge, the reality still feeling a little raw. I'm glad if I can help Max find a part of himself he's never known about. But, if I'm being honest, I'm crazy jealous of whoever will reap the benefits.

Beck's eyes widen. "Oh my god, I told you he had a thing for you."

"No, sweetie," I shake my head sadly. "He was into the idea of bondage. He asked all these questions about it, like where to learn how to do it and stuff. So now he's going to turn from a sexy straight boy, to a *kinky* sexy straight boy. He's going to find some gorgeous, kinky woman, and they'll live kinkily ever after."

"Deep breaths, babe," Beck suggests, rubbing my

back.

"You take deep breaths," I snap an immature comeback, and Beck chuckles at me.

"Good one. Hey, why don't you come out to O'Malley's tonight? Gage and I are going out with all the guys. Invite Max if you want. You need some serious unwinding."

"Trust me, a drink isn't the kind of unwinding I need," I mutter.

"Sorry, can't help you there."

"Yeah, apparently no one can," I groan in full on pity party mode now.

"He's out there dude. My money is still on Max, but if not him, then someone. Your perfect, kinky, sweet man is right around the corner."

"Well, if you can tell me which corner, it would really speed this process up."

"I know, babe. I wish I could tell you where to find Mr. Right. What I can tell you, though, is that it's *so* worth the wait once you find him."

I sigh at the dreamy look that comes over Beck's face. I want what he has with Gage. Beck's man accepts all his makeup and lace happily and loves him even more for it. *That's* what I need. I need a man who will love me inside and out and love me even more for my bondage kink. Not like I'm asking much.

"Yeah, I'll come tonight, and I'll invite Max."

"Yay!" Beck claps his hands enthusiastically.

"Now go do something useful so I have time to get paperwork and shit done." I wave him off and head for the stack of stuff piling up in my office. I will admit the one thing I didn't count on when opening a business was that I'd have a lot more paperwork and a lot less time to dance.

I pull out my phone and text Max with an invite for tonight, and he responds ten minutes later agreeing to meet at the bar down the street from Heathens Ink where Beck's boyfriend and all his friends work.

Max

I stared at Clay's text for ten minutes before agreeing to go to the bar tonight with Beck's friends.

It's nothing out of the ordinary. We go to O'Malley's at least twice a month with the tattoo artists from Heathens. Sometimes a cop named Cas joins us and moons over the bartender—Beau—he's banging. All of this is average in my life. So why am I suddenly hesitant?

Maybe because spending the night with a bunch of gay couples is a little too strange right now when I'm crushing on Clay?

Am I crushing on Clay?

I let out a frustrated breath as I replace the spark plugs on the Chevy I'm working on.

I already decided I can't be crushing on Clay because I'm straight. And straight guys don't just wake up gay one day. That's not how things work. You know you're gay from like birth or whatever.

I pull out my phone and type a quick text, telling Clay I'm in for tonight. Hanging out with a bunch of gay couples didn't *turn* me gay. I'm being ridiculous, and I need to knock it off already. Maybe I can even find a woman who'll catch my attention at the bar tonight and then I'll prove to myself that I like women as much as I always have.

Besides, I could use a night of fun before I have to go talk to Jess tomorrow.

###

After work, I ride my bike home and jump in the shower to get ready to go out.

The hot water cascades over my tight muscles, and my mind betrays me by conjuring up the image of Clay, wondering how beautiful his tattoos must look as the water runs over them.

My chest heaves, and I don't even bother to shake off the image for a handful of heartbeats: Clay with his hair wet and his skin pink under the hot stream of water. In my mind, Clay lowers himself to his knees and looks up at me with longing. My hand travels toward my aching cock before I realize what I'm doing and hurriedly shut off the water.

I jump out of the shower and reach for a towel. I dry myself off quickly, avoiding my cock, which hasn't gotten the message and is still hard as stone. I am *not* going to jerk off thinking about my best friend...again.

I wrap the towel around my waist and pull open the bathroom door in a rush, needing to get to my room and put my clothes on immediately. My body smacks against a smaller mass, and I freeze when Clay's hands come up and brace against my stomach. My skin tingles at every point of contact with his smooth fingertips.

Please don't let him notice me tenting the towel.

"Sorry," Clay blushes and steps back and then out of my way.

"It's fine," I grunt, hurrying to put him behind me before he can realize how painfully hard I am.

It's not until pulling on my pants that I realize Clay was supposed to meet me at the bar, not at home.

I open my door and call out to Clay who appears from his own room a few seconds later.

"What's up?" Clay asks.

"What are you doing home? I thought I was meeting you at the bar?"

"Yeah, I spilled coffee on my shirt, so I needed to come home and change."

I catch Clay's eyes roaming over my chest and realize I haven't pulled a shirt on yet. To my surprise, his gaze on my bare skin is like a caress. His tongue swipes along his bottom lip and makes my cock hard all over again. My body is trembling, desperate to reach for him and...I'm not sure what exactly, except in my mind there's a lot of skin-to-skin contact.

I bite back a groan at the images flashing through my mind. "Uh, I'd better finish getting ready," I mumble before stumbling backward into my room again.

I unbutton my pants and adjust my erection so it's less painful, unable to resist a few slow strokes. I don't know why I'm teasing myself when I know I don't have time to jerk off. Not to mention, I'm not going to let myself get off to Clay. *I won't.*

A few minutes later there's a tentative knock at my door.

"You almost ready?"

"Yeah, here I come," I call back, taking a deep breath and trying to focus on a clear mind.

When we get to O'Malley's, all the other guys are already there.

The first time I met the crew from Heathens, I didn't really know how to take them. They're a tight-knit group, and it's intimidating as hell, and I was surprised to see them welcome me into their close family unit. Over the past year since Beck and Gage have been together, I've gotten to know these guys better, even if I do feel like I stick out like a sore thumb being the only straight guy here. Beck waves Clay and me over to the tables they've grabbed in the corner of the bar.

"You go, I'll grab a couple drinks for us," I offer.

"Thanks, I'll get the next round."

As Clay walks away, my eyes find his tight, round ass, and my stomach flips and aches with longing before I tear my eyes away and head to the bar.

"Hey there, how're you doin' tonight?" the bartender, Beau, greets me with a bright smile.

"I'm good, how about you?"

"Can't complain," he shrugs and chuckles.

It's common knowledge that all the guys—plus the only woman who works at Heathens, Dani—

all think Beau is a total hottie. I take a second to assess him. If I'm suddenly gay, I should want to jump this guy, that much I'm sure of.

He's certainly attractive, with shaggy blond hair and piercing blue eyes. Plus, he's got fantastic ink covering his arms, which is always a turn on. Not to mention his pouty lips and a killer smile. He's good looking; there's no denying that. But, I don't have the urge to drag him to my bedroom and have my way with him like I've been having toward Clay.

"Can I get you anything?" Beau prompts after what I'm sure was a long awkward silence while I checked him out.

"Two rum and cokes."

Beau turns to grab the drinks and a hulking form appears beside me.

"You checking out my man?" Cas accuses with narrowed eyes.

My own eyes go wide as I grapple for a defense. I *was* checking out Beau, and I am so busted.

"I, uh..."

Cas' serious expression morphs into a smile, and then he starts to laugh.

"I'm just fucking with you. Beau is hot as fuck, look all you want. Hell, we're open so feel free to do more than look if he's into it."

"Uh..."

"Wait, aren't you straight?" Cas cocks his head and examines me.

"Yeah, I'm straight," I confirm with less confidence

in my tone than I would've liked when answering that question. "I was just...checking."

Cas' smile softens.

"Sometimes being bi is a lot harder than being gay, I think. You know you're attracted to women and that's so much easier than taking a deeper look at your sexuality."

"Thanks, but I don't think I am—bi that is."

"Okay. I am, and so are Beau, Adam, Royal, Nash, and Owen. If you ever wanted to talk more about it with anyone, we're here."

I nod and accept the drinks from Beau when he returns. I throw down a generous tip and then head over to the table where Clay is waiting for his drink.

Could Cas be right? Maybe I'm bi? But that still doesn't explain why it would take me until thirty-two years old to figure it out. It's more likely the kink, which makes the most sense.

Around the table, there's a spate of happy couples —or trio in one case. I've never been obsessed with relationships or anything, but in the last year or two, I've noticed a certain longing surprising me every once in a while. It would be nice to have someone to come home to every night, to share my days with, to share my *life* with. They would have to love Gigi as much as I do, of course.

"Hey, Max, you have any ink?" Royal asks from his place between his two men, Nash and Zade.

"No, he doesn't," Clay answers for me and then blushes like he'd admitted more than he intended to.

"How do you know? Maybe I've got a secret tat on my ass," I joke.

"Sorry dude, but I've seen your ass." Clay smirks at me over the rim of his glass and something warm settles over me.

"No, I don't have any ink. Why?" I ask Royal.

"He loves inking virgins, so he's trying to drum someone up," Nash explains with a smirk.

"Oh, actually there is a tattoo I've wanted for a while. I've been psyching myself up for it."

"Hell yeah, come by this week, and I will hook you up," Royal declares.

"Okay, I'm sold. I'll come in Wednesday."

At the far end of the table, I catch Adam smiling as he watches Beck sitting on Gage's lap, the two of them lost in conversation and each other's eyes.

The only single guy, aside from Clay and me, is Owen. He's sitting two seats down from me, looking content as can be among all the couples.

Then there's Madden and Thane, sitting beside Adam and Nox, talking about the headache of planning a wedding.

"It's not too late for us to tie the knot in Vegas when we go next month," Thane suggests, and Madden rolls his eyes. This is clearly a well-trodden argument between the men.

"I planned this damn wedding, and we're not blowing it off."

"Anything you want, sweetheart." Thane kisses Madden on the side of the head and Madden smiles.

"You think I'll ever find someone who'll love me like that?" Clay asks with a sigh, clearly watching Madden and Thane as well.

"Absolutely. You're a catch, dude." I put my hand on his knee and give it a light squeeze to reassure him, but the gesture causes both of us to tense.

It's not like I've ever shied away from touching Clay, but this feels different for some reason. Everything feels different lately.

"Thanks," he says, licking his lips and shifting in his seat.

I pull my hand back and reach for my drink, taking a big gulp to chase away the awkward moment hanging in the air between us.

"Oh hey, I've been meaning to ask if you already planned something for Gigi's birthday in two weeks?" Clay asks, instantly bringing us back into familiar territory.

"I had a few ideas, but I'm open to suggestions."

"The Burke Museum has a butterfly dome exhibit going on right now. I thought that would be something she'd really like."

"That's perfect, she'd love that. She loves the dinosaur stuff there, too. You going to come with us?"

"Of course. Like I'd let you take all the credit for my favorite girl's birthday?"

"Touché," I laugh.

CHAPTER 11

Max

Saturday morning finds me standing on Jess' doorstep, waiting for her to answer my knock.

I've gone over what I want to say a thousand times in my mind this week. The last thing I want to do is blow up at her and make things worse.

The more I've thought about it all week, the more certain I am that I can't live with the thought of only seeing Gigi two months of the year. I don't know what the solution is, but I absolutely can't live that way.

The door opens, and I find myself looking at a well-coiffed, dark haired man. It's a Saturday morning at eight o'clock, but he's clearly showered, shaved, and carefully chosen his clothes for the day. If I were at home, I'd still be in my pajamas.

"You must be Mark?" I hold out my hand in greeting.

"I am. And I'm assuming you're Max?"

His handshake is a little too firm—like he thinks he's going to intimidate me. Poor guy has no idea who he's dealing with. I squeeze back and fix him with a leveling look.

"Is Jess around? I need to talk to her for a minute

before I take my daughter for the weekend."

"Yes, come in." He steps aside, and I enter the house.

"Daddy!" Gigi comes flying down the stairs and jumps into my arms with barely enough warning to catch her.

"We talked about this, princess. You've gotta give me warning before you do that, I don't want to drop you."

"Clay doesn't need warning," she argues.

"Fine, don't come crying to me if he ever drops you."

"Daddy," she whines, and I chuckle.

"I have to talk to your mom real quick, why don't you get your shoes on, and make sure you have anything you need for the weekend, and then we'll go soon."

I set her down and follow the sound of Jess and Mark's voices to the kitchen.

"Can we talk for a second, Jess?"

"Of course, have a seat," she offers, pointing at the chair opposite the one she's sitting in at the kitchen table.

"I want us to go to mediation to work something out with Gigi."

Jess sighs and gives me a pitying look.

"Max, I know I should've handled it differently rather than just springing it on you. But, there are no good compromises. I'm willing to give you Christmas and Spring break in addition to her Summer breaks from school. I don't see what more I can do aside from that."

"And what about in a few years when she has friends she doesn't want to be away from all summer?" I challenge, my throat tight and my fists clenching in frustration. "She's my daughter; you can't just take her from me like this."

"I'm not trying to take her from you. I wish Mark and I didn't have to move, but life doesn't always work out the way you plan. I'm sorry, but we *are* moving to New York, and Gigi is coming with us."

My chest heaves with restraint. My brain recognizes the rationality of everything Jess is saying, but my heart won't accept it. I can feel my baby girl slipping through my fingers. Sure, maybe I'll get all her school breaks for the next year or two, but before long, she won't want to leave her friends she'll make in New York, and then when will I see her? It'll just be a phone call once a month.

"Daddy, what's wrong?" Gigi asks, coming into the kitchen and stopping in her tracks when she sees how upset I am.

"Nothing, princess," I assure her with a smile, forcing my rampaging emotions down to be dealt with later. "You ready to go?"

"Yeah," she nods, holding up her pink backpack to show me she's got everything she needs.

"See you Monday after school, sweetie," Jess says, pulling Gigi into a hug.

"Call me if you need anything, Max, or if you want to continue this conversation later."

I grunt and nod, not trusting myself to speak to Jess when my emotions are this close to the surface.

Clay

I pull a tray of fresh baked chocolate chip cookies out of the oven a few seconds before the front door opens, and Gigi comes barreling into the kitchen.

"Whoa, hold on tornado child," I warn when she reaches for a cookie. "They're still hot; you'll have to wait a few minutes."

Her face falls, and I have to admit, the girl's got a killer puppy dog face.

"Do I smell cookies?" Max asks, coming into the kitchen with a boyish, hopeful smile.

"Yes, but they just came out of the oven, so you need to wait a few minutes."

Max's face falls in the same way Gigi's did and my heart warms. Those two are too damn cute for words.

"If you want, G, I'll paint your nails while you wait for the cookies to cool?"

"I don't like nail polish anymore," she informs me in a haughty tone.

"Oh, well excuse me," I return her tone, and Max grins at us.

"Can I go play on my tablet for a little while?" she asks her dad.

"Sure thing, princess."

Gigi races off, and I start to clean up the mess I made while preparing the cookies.

"I talked to Jess," Max says, his tone dejected, which makes me want to hug all his problems away.

"She didn't agree to mediation?"

"She said it wouldn't change anything. My brain knows she's right, but what am I supposed to do? I can't lose Gigi."

"I know." I crouch down beside Max, sitting in a chair at the kitchen table. "There has to be a solution. We'll figure this out."

Max doesn't look convinced, but he nods and then pulls me into a hug that surprises as much as it pleases me. I don't understand what's been going on with him the past few days. But he's my best friend, and I'm going to help him figure all this stuff out.

Max

The weekend passed uneventfully, and I gave Gigi an extra hug Monday morning before Clay took her to school.

Ever since my conversation with Jess, I've been restless and agitated, and I'm certain it has everything to do with how helpless this situation has made me. My daughter is slipping away, and there's no way I can hang on to her.

"Hey bro, my friend Ace was asking about you," Tony tells me when I walk into the shop Wednesday morning.

"What about?"

"He saw your Tumblr page with the classic bikes

you restore. He's got a motorcycle shop; they repair classics and build custom," Tony explains.

"Oh yeah, where at?" I ask, my interest more than piqued. That sounds like exactly the kind of place I've been dreaming of working.

"Out in Philly."

I roll my eyes at my brother.

"Thanks for getting my hopes up for nothing, dude." I shoot him the finger and then shoulder past him to get to work.

On the bright side, I have my tattoo to look forward to this afternoon.

I show up at Heathens still sweaty and greasy from work, but I figure Royal won't mind too much. I meant to go home and shower first, but I got absorbed rebuilding an engine and lost track of time. Nox is sitting at the front desk when I walk in.

"Hi, Max. Royal's waiting for you, you can head straight toward the back; his studio is the second on the left."

"Thanks." I give him a friendly nod and head in the direction he indicated.

"Hey, man," Royal greets me with a pat on the shoulder. "I've got everything all set for your tat. I just need to know where we're putting this beauty."

I glance at the image Royal created for me after I sent him an email about what I was looking for. And tears well up in my eyes.

I'd been planning to get a tattoo of Gigi's baby footprints since she was born, but now seems like the perfect time.

"Over my heart," I tell him without hesitation.

"Cool, lose the shirt and we'll get started."

I strip my t-shirt over my head and toss it on a nearby chair.

"Damn, all that manual labor has done you a lot of favors," Royal comments, not bothering to hide his perusal of my bare chest and abs. I blush and squirm a little under his gaze.

"Babe, I thought we talked about this. You're not supposed to hit on straight boys; it scares them," Nash admonishes from the doorway of Royal's workspace.

"Hey, it worked on you," Royal argues with a smirk.

"But I wasn't straight, I just didn't know I was bi yet at the time."

That grabs my attention. I can't imagine going from not knowing you like guys to being in a relationship with two men at once.

"How does that work, exactly? You never once thought about a guy sexually, and then one day you just woke up and hopped in bed with two of them?"

Royal and Nash both laugh. "Yup, he just climbed right in there."

"Not exactly," Nash corrects. "I think it wasn't part of myself that I was ready to acknowledge before then, but in hindsight, there were clues that I was attracted to men, specifically to Royal. At the time, I guess I saw it as normal affection for my best bro? It sounds absurd now because it should've been a major red flag that I consistently chose hanging out with Royal over dating and getting laid."

"Huh." I keep my face carefully neutral, but inside my head, my thoughts are raging. Why does Nash's story have to hit so close to home? Am I bisexual? I certainly have feelings for Clay, as difficult as they've been to process.

"Mind if I sit in here while Royal works? I get lonely in my workspace all by myself."

"That's fine." My mind is running over everything Nash just said and slowly slotting pieces into place.

"So, you're bi, too Royal?" I ask as Royal whips out a razor and starts to shave a patch on my chest to work.

"Yup. I'm more into guys, though. Which I think is why I realized it a lot sooner than Nash. He mostly likes women, so his attraction to men was easy for him to overlook for a long time."

I hum in response, too many emotions swirling through me to sort out.

I can feel Nash's eyes on me, studying my face. I wonder what he's finding there. Is it written all over my expression that I'm confused, afraid, and maybe a little hopeful?

"It was confusing as hell at first," Nash goes on. "I'd always loved Royal as a friend, so it wasn't a difficult adjustment to realize I loved him in even more ways. But it surprised the hell out of me to realize how attractive I found Zade. That's what really threw me, if I'm being honest."

I swallow hard and nod. "Were you worried at all that you were wrong about your attraction? Like, what if you *thought* you were into Royal and Zade and then you made a move and realize it didn't do anything for you? That would ruin a friendship, don't you think?" I ask, certain Nash and Royal will both see through my convoluted question.

"Yeah, I was nervous as hell," Nash says. "But there gets to be a certain point where the attraction is undeniable. I just had to look past my own preconceived ideas and fears, and then I *knew* without a shadow of a doubt."

My gut tightens, and my heart races in my chest. Could I look past my own expectations and fears to see if what I feel for Clay could be real, be more?

I can't find any words to respond as Royal presses the outline to my skin and then gets to work, inking my baby's footprints permanently over my heart.

Over the next few hours while he works, I observe Royal and Nash together. Every look they cast in each other's direction, the little jokes they share together, and the look on both their faces when they talk about their other man, Zade. All of it adds up to one undeniable truth.

I want what they have.

I want someone who completes me the way they complete each other. I want someone who puts that kind of smile on my face. I want someone to love and cherish. And if that person just so happens to be Clay, should I risk letting that slip through my fingers just because he's not what I expected?

CHAPTER 12

Clay

Big: Hi, I'd love to hear more about the bondage thing

I let out a sigh and delete the message from the very cleverly named *Big*. Beck tried to tell me I'd never find the right guy on Grindr or any other dating app, and I refused to accept that at first. But now I'm too tired to keep pushing for something that obviously isn't there. I don't know where the right guy is, but he's not on Grindr.

I hear the front door open, and my heart flutters a little.

Max's newfound interest in bondage hasn't done anything to help the hopeless crush I have on him. *Go figure.*

Max appears with a smile and a strange look in his eyes.

"Hey, love, how'd your first tattoo go?"

"Fantastic. I should've gotten this done years ago," Max says as he pulls off his shirt to show me his new ink.

I gulp at the sight of his hard abs and lickable happy trail.

He peels off the bandage, and I admire the precious replica of Gigi's baby footprints right over his heart.

"It's perfect," I smile.

"Yeah," he agrees, looking at me in a way that heats my face. "Hey, you want to hang out tonight? We could watch a movie or something?"

"Yeah, that sounds good. Why don't I fix us up some dinner, and then we can watch some movies or pick a show on Netflix."

"Sounds good, I'm just going to take a quick shower first."

"Okay. Your tattoo will sting in the water so try to avoid getting it directly under the stream. Wash it very gently with unscented soap, and be sure to pat it dry after rather than rubbing it dry."

"Got it. Thanks." And then to my surprise, Max gives me a quick kiss on the cheek before disappearing down the hall.

What the hell has gotten into him?

Max

The feel of Clay's body shifting beside mine sends little electric jolts up my spine and straight to my balls. My body drifts closer to Clay's unconsciously. I want to feel his body heat, feel him in my personal space.

I don't know what's happening to me, but after talking to Nash today, I can't stop wondering. It's possible it's the kink. Is it so crazy I'd be attracted to the idea of having total control over something, even for just a few minutes? Or maybe it's Nash's words getting to me about how he never realized he was into guys until he fell for Royal and Zade. Looking at those guys, so insanely in love, I can't imagine them not finding each other in the way they have. What if Nash had been too afraid to take the risk to see where his unexpected feelings would lead?

I turn my head and let myself take him in. He *is* undeniably attractive. His eyes are captivating, his lips are full and enticing, and his small frame is just right to fold into my arms. But there's nothing feminine about him. He's all lines and edges and...*hair*. I swallow hard as my cock shifts against my thigh. I don't understand why, and maybe I don't have to understand. Maybe—for right now—this is what feels right.

Clay must feel my eyes on him because he turns and cocks his head.

"What?"

What?

Oh nothing, just imagining tying you to your bedframe and using my tongue on every inch of your body.

"What?" I ask back, feigning ignorance.

"Why are you looking at me like a weirdo?"

My tongue sweeps out to wet my lips as the words try to arrange themselves in my mind. How do I even broach this subject? What if it's not what Clay is even looking for? Maybe I'm not his type, and I'm just here obsessing over something that's never going to happen. So what if he thinks I'm hot? That doesn't mean he wants me to do any of the things I'm suddenly imagining.

Testing the waters, I move one hand down to rest on the back of Clay's neck. He stills, holding his breath and looking into my eyes like he's searching for answers.

When he relaxes into my touch, I assume he found whatever he was looking for. I put the slightest bit of pressure on the back of his neck, and I lean in— slowly at first and then all at once.

Clay's lips are soft and pliable against mine, and when his tongue sweeps out to meet mine, we both shudder.

Again, there's no pretending I'm kissing a woman. His short hair tickles my hand, a little bit of rough stubble rubbing against my chin. And, to my surprise, I don't want to pretend he's a woman. I don't want to pretend it's anyone but Clay.

Our lips and tongues continue to duel as Clay leans back, taking me along with him until I'm covering his body.

Without a thought, I grab Clay's wrists tightly in one hand and hold them above his head and trap his legs between mine. It's not ropes or handcuffs, but it seems to work well enough as Clay stills beneath me and lets out a little whimper between panting breaths.

"Oh god, Max, please," he rasps. I expect him to follow it up with something crude, like a request to jerk him off. But, instead… "Tell me what this is."

"What?"

"Is this a like an experiment for you or are you suddenly into guys? And will this ruin our friendship?"

"If I promise it won't ruin our friendship, can I tell you I don't have an answer to the first part yet?"

Clay bites down on his bottom lip and squirms beneath me for a second before sighing. "I guess that'll do for now."

I attack his mouth again and tighten my grip on his wrists as he relaxes into my hold. Clay's hard cock nudges against my stomach through his sweatpants and a groan escapes from deep in my chest.

I've always liked the way a woman fits against me all soft and warm. But there's no deny-ing how good a man's body feels. Not just any man's body—Clay's body. I grind our bodies to-gether, my own erection pressed against the in-side of Clay's thigh.

We moan and gasp against each other's lips as the tension builds. I never thought that in my early thirties I'd be able to get off rubbing fully clothed up against another man. But it's going to happen, and I'm not even sorry about it.

"Clay, *Clay*," I grit out his name, and I feel him shudder beneath me before his whole body tenses, and his eyes flutter shut.

"God, Max."

When I feel the wet spot through his pants, my body heats, and my balls draw tight.

I huff and grunt as I fuck myself against Clay, trapped beneath me and mine for the taking. My generous, confident best friend who just came, gasping my name.

I don't stop until my own pants are sticky, and my balls are empty.

Clay shudders again when I release his wrists. His body starts to tremble a little, so I lay down next to him and pull him against my chest.

"Hey, are you okay?" I ask gently.

"Yeah, sorry, that was intense."

Intense is an understatement. That was earth shattering, life changing.

"We can do this again, right?" I ask.

Clay's breath tickles my neck as he laughs.

"You're the straight guy. If you're not endlessly freaked out, I'm certainly not going to turn down the chance to be your quarter life crisis."

"You're not a crisis."

"What am I?"

"You're my best friend."

I wake up feeling lighter than I have since…I honestly can't even remember. Images of the night before with Clay on the couch flash through my mind and set my blood on fire.

I still don't understand *what* this is. What I do

know is something about it feels so right. How long have I loved Clay as a best friend? *Years.* Is it so strange that something else could develop?

If you ask guys like my brothers, I'm sure it *would* seem crazy. But it's not like I'm suddenly gay...at least, I don't think I am. I don't understand much of what's happening except to know that I want to explore it and see where it leads.

I hear the floorboards in the hallway creak, and I can't stop the smile that spreads across my lips. Just the thought of Clay makes me a little giddy. *Yeah, this is worth exploring.*

I slip out of bed and tug on a pair of pants and run my fingers through my long hair to untangle it just enough to be presentable. And then I take a deep breath and venture out to find Clay.

When I reach the kitchen, I find Clay standing over the sink, washing the dishes from the night before, and another smile tugs at my lips. He's kind of cute when he's stressed, and now I know the secret to unraveling all the tension he carries around.

The thought sends heat spiking through me.

My eyes roam over his tight little ass in his yoga pants and over the beautiful wild flower sleeves inked on both his arms. *How did I never notice before how sexy he is?* Maybe it's like Nash said; I wasn't ready before now. Hell, I'm not sure I'm ready now. But maybe I can get there? Maybe we can try?

Clay shuts off the sink and turns around, startling when he sees me.

"Jeez, how long have you been standing there?" he asks putting a hand over his heart like I nearly gave him a heart attack.

"Only a second."

"Oh." Clay forces a smile and then shifts awkwardly on his feet before reaching for the coffee pot to start coffee.

"Let me get that," I offer, taking a tentative step forward.

"Thanks."

Clay continues to stand like he's a stranger in our kitchen while I add the water and grounds to the machine.

"So, last night was fun," I venture, hoping like hell he feels the same way.

I can hear the breath whoosh out of his lungs and see his shoulders relax out of the corner of my eye.

"Yeah, it was. If you, uh, ever want to do it again, you know where to find me."

"I do," I blurt and then cringe internally at how desperate I sound. Fuck it, I don't want to leave this shit nebulous. "I want to do it again, as long as you want to. I've been watching some videos—bondage videos—and I'd like to try."

"Yeah," Clay agrees in a shaky voice. "Yeah, that would be good."

"Okay," I nod and bite down on my bottom lip to contain my enthusiasm. "I'd better shower and get to work, but I'll see you tonight?"

"I live here, so yeah."

I chuckle and then, without giving it any thought,

I grab Clay by the waist and plant a brief kiss against his lips.

"Ha-have a good day," he stutters when I release him.

"You too, petal."

CHAPTER 13

Clay

"Clay," Beck says my name with frustration and snaps his fingers in my face.

"Sorry, what?" I blink away my muddled thoughts and try to focus on whatever Beck is trying to talk to me about.

I still can't believe last night happened. I've imagined Max's lips and body a thousand times, but god that was *so* much better than I ever thought it could be. I fully expected a total straight guy freak out afterward or this morning at the least. Somehow, he seems okay with everything. More than okay. He seems eager to go another round tonight. My body flares to life remembering his words this morning. *I've been watching some videos—bondage videos—and I'd like to try.* I shift, hoping my growing erection isn't too noticeable in my yoga pants. There's a pipedream if I've ever heard one.

"Clay, what the hell is up with you this morning?" Beck asks, putting his hands on his hips and squinting at me.

Shit, I wasn't listening again.

I bite down on my bottom lip as I try to decide if Max would be okay with me telling Beck what happened. Then again, Beck is my best friend, so Max should expect that I'd tell him.

"Something happened last night with Max."

"What?" Beck gasps, a look of delight creeping over his face. "Oh my god, tell me everything right this second."

"Dude, I'm not telling you *everything*," I laugh as a giddy lightness fills me.

"Holy shit, are you saying what I think you're saying?"

"I'll tell you this much; the man knows how to kiss. And, this morning he made a point of saying he wants to spend time together tonight."

"Oh. My. God!" Beck squeals and starts to jump up and down. I laugh at my best friend's enthusiasm until he forces me to jump up and down with him and then do a little dance.

When we finally calm down, I force myself to voice what's nagging at the back of my mind. "I'm sure this is a phase or an experiment, though. I don't want to get overly excited when it won't last. I'm going to enjoy it while I can and then move on with dignity when Max remembers he's not gay."

Beck rolls his eyes at me.

"That boy has been in love with you for years."

"No, he's not," I argue, shielding my heart from the hope Beck's words threaten to instill there.

When I get home from work, I half expect Max to

have finally realized what happened last night and have a delayed freak out. I wouldn't blame him. If I woke up one day and realized I fooled around with a woman, I'd be a little weirded out. Not that there's anything wrong with women, it's just not within the framework of how I see myself. Even if Max is just now discovering he's bi, it can take a lot of adjusting to realize you aren't the same person you always saw yourself as.

I step through the door and find Max waiting for me on the couch with a smile.

"Hey, how was your day?" he asks.

"Kind of stressful," I admit. "I'm trying to figure out what classes to offer for the spring, and it takes a lot of guesswork and projections to figure out what will likely bring in the most students."

"I guess I'll have to help you relax," Max suggests with heat in his voice that gets my dick instantly hard.

Okay, so not freaking out apparently.

"Where are your manners?" I tease. "At least buy me dinner first."

"That's fair," Max agrees. "Where do you want to go?"

I shrug. "I'm not picky, you can decide."

"I know seafood is out," Max notes my distaste of fish, and I smile.

I've had men think they're going to get in my pants showing their Dom side, starting with telling me what I'm going to order at a restaurant. That's a quick deal breaker. But, Max knows me well enough that I'd let him order for me. In fact, it might be a little hot coming from Max.

"I'll go get changed real quick and then we can go out."

Max nods, and I pause for a second wondering if I should clarify whether this is a date or not. He didn't say it was a date. But it *is* a meal prior to sex, which in my book is a date. I decide to keep it casual since Max is wearing jeans and a t-shirt.

After I pull on some clothes and make sure my hair looks okay, I head back out to find Max waiting for me with one of his spare motorcycle jackets and helmet.

"What's that for?" I eye the accoutrements with suspicion.

"No arguing; I'm taking you on my bike." His tone is firm and sexy as hell, but I'm still unsure about the idea of riding on a motorcycle. "You trust me?"

That question breaks down my defenses, and my shoulders sag in defeat. "Of course, I do, you big dope."

Max smiles like a little kid, and I laugh and shake my head at him.

He offers me the jacket and helmet and then leads me outside.

Max swings his leg over his beast of a bike and then crooks his finger at me.

"Get on, petal."

I take a deep breath and then square my shoulders before clumsily clamoring onto the back of the bike. I press my body flush against Max's back and wrap my arms tightly around his midsection. Okay, maybe I can see *some* of the appeal here.

The bike roars to life beneath us, and the vibrations between my thighs make me gasp. *Yeah, I'm totally getting this now*.

We jolt forward, and I squeeze Max harder, closing my eyes and praying he doesn't get us killed.

Max

I chuckle to myself as I bring the bike to a stop at the bar and grill I decided to take Clay to, and his grip around my waist doesn't ease immediately. There's no better first date move than a motorcycle ride. Not that Clay and I are on a date. Or maybe we are. I'm not entirely sure, and I don't think I'm ready to think all that hard about it.

For now, all I want is to take my best friend out to dinner and then go home and see about exploring whatever this unexpected spark is between us.

"We're here," I inform Clay with amusement.

He peeks an eye open and loosens his grip a fraction. "We didn't die?"

I scoff and pull my helmet off. "That would be a pretty dumb move on my part to get us killed before I've had my way with you."

"Good point," Clay agrees before removing

his own helmet and stumbling off the bike. I catch him before he can faceplant.

Once he's steady on his feet again, I'm reluctant to let him go. But one glance around tells me it's a busy Thursday night downtown, and I'm not ready to be seen in public feeling up my very male roommate.

Clay seems to understand, taking one step back and giving me a reassuring smile.

We head into the restaurant with my heart thundering in my ears. I'm not sure why I'm nervous. It's not like Clay and I haven't hung out like this thousands of times. This is different though. This time, I know what his lips taste like and what he sounds like when he comes apart. This time, there's a possibility of taking him home to strip him naked and lick all his soft skin. This time, he's so much more than my bro.

Once we're seated, we manage to fall into normal conversation about work and Gigi. It's nothing more than a night out with my best friend —the person who knows me better than anyone in the world. Except with every shy glance and bump of our knees under the table, I know it's so much more than that. I *need* it to be so much more than that.

After dinner, I take the long way home, enjoying the feel of Clay clinging to me far too much to give it up quickly.

As we ride through the city, I wonder what it would be like to date a man. What would my brothers and my dad think? What would Gigi think? She loves Clay; I'm sure it wouldn't faze her. Hell, as far as I know she already assumes that Clay and I are together. It's not like a kid can tell the difference anyway.

By the time we pull into our driveway, Clay is finally relaxing a bit on the back of the bike. I bet I'll be able to lure him out again, now that he's seen that it's not as scary as he imagined. There are hundreds of places I could drive us just to feel the wind on our skin and his arms around my middle.

Once we're inside, I follow Clay to the kitchen where he pulls out a couple of drinks, and we sit down at the table.

"Thanks for dinner," he says as he taps his fingers along the neck of the beer bottle.

"My pleasure," I assure him. "You know I like spending time with you."

Clay nods and fidgets and shifts in his seat before standing up and grabbing a rag to wipe down the counter.

He's wound so tight he looks like he's about to snap. Something surges inside me, demanding that I take care of him. I can calm all the anxiety inside of him, at least for as long as I can keep him bound and focusing only on pleasure.

I swallow around the lump in my throat. This is a step up from some kissing and grinding. Am I ready?

Clay turns and faces me. When our eyes meet, a spike of longing jolts me, and it's all I can do not to take him here on the kitchen floor.

I stand and close the distance between us in two long strides.

Clay's breath catches as I place my hand under his chin and tilt his face upward. I run my thumb along the rough stubble on his jaw, and we both shudder.

Clay's lips part, and his body sways toward me. A surge of lust hits me in the pit of my stomach and steals my breath.

"I want you so badly," I whisper almost in wonder. I've never felt this way toward *anyone* before.

"Let's go to my bedroom," Clay suggests breathlessly.

I nod and then bend forward to brush my lips against his. Clay clutches the front of my shirt and melts against me. I take the opportunity to stoop down and grasp the back of his thighs, hoisting him up against me with ease.

Clay laughs and tightens his grip around my neck.

"I'm not going to drop you, petal," I assure him.

"Why are you calling me that?"

"Petal? Like flower petal," I explain with a pointed glance at his wildflower tattoos covering his arms.

A mixture of confusion and soft hope pass through his eyes before he kisses me again.

I manage to make it to his bedroom without breaking the kiss or bumping into any walls along the way. I lower Clay to his bed, reluctant to let him out of my arms.

I gaze down at Clay, trembling and panting already before I've even touched him.

"Is this what you want?" I check, running the back of my hand along his cheek.

"Yes," Clay answers instantly. "I want it so much I'm not sure I even have enough words to tell you."

I chuckle. "That's okay, just relax and let me take care of you."

Clay whimpers and nods.

My own hands are unsteady as I strip Clay's shirt over his head and then work on his pants.

I know Clay said he doesn't like to be submissive, but he seems more than content to lay panting as I strip him bare before me.

"Can you put your arms above your head for me?" I ask gently, conscious of the fact that Clay told me the other men he tried to play with were too dominating. I don't need to dominate him; I just need to bring him pleasure.

Clay shivers a little and slowly lifts his arms over his head.

I take a deep breath and hope I'm able to bind him the way he likes. My eyes roam over his body, spread out and trembling for me. There's no denying all his hard lines and dark body hair are in sharp contrast to what I've always considered arousing. But my cock is hard, pulsing in the confines of my jeans. All I want to do is lick and touch every inch of him. I want him gasping and writhing under my caress. I want to see what his face looks like when he comes again.

"Don't move," I request before turning and heading to Clay's closet to grab the ropes I discovered there the other day.

I revel again at the soft bindings against my calloused hands.

"I read online that I should have safety scissors, just in case. Do you have any?"

"Top drawer of my nightstand." Clay points and I open the drawer to find a pair of sturdy scissors beside condoms and lube. I set the scissors on top of the stand so they'll be easily accessible if needed.

I return to where Clay is splayed out on the bed and tease the rope against his skin. He shudders as goosebumps erupt all over his skin, and he arches toward me.

Clay lets out a quiet whimper as I start to twine the soft rope around his biceps, trying to gauge the right amount of slack to leave to ensure he's comfortable but properly restrained. I want to do this right for him. I don't know why it's so important to me, but I don't want him left feeling disappointed.

I force my fingers to stay steady as I work the rope up his arms, nimbly weaving it around each arm in a simple design.

I saw so many pictures of mind blowing artwork created in the binding, but I'll have to work up to that level. This is just a crisscross to lock his arms together, and then I loop the rope through the slats on the headboard and secure them.

Once he's in place, I glance at his face,

to make sure he's not showing pain from being bound too tightly. On the contrary, his expression is somewhere between bliss and utter relaxation. The usual furrow in his brow is smooth, and his jaw is slack.

Pride rushes through me. I'm already giving Clay what he needs, and it's only going to get better.

Once I'm satisfied that his hands are secure, I go back for two of the remaining lengths of rope and then bind each of his legs to the baseboard, spread wide so I'll be able to kneel between his legs.

Clay's chest rises and falls rapidly, his eyes closed, and his cheeks are beautifully flushed. I've never seen anything sexier in my life, and I haven't even touched him yet. If there was any doubt that Clay gets off on the binding itself, that's gone now. I'll have to remember next time to spend more time on the binding process to build his pleasure higher. And there's no question, there *will* be a next time.

I climb onto the bed and kneel between his spread legs. I place one of my rough hands on his throat, not applying pressure, simply feeling his pulse against my palm.

My other hand roams over Clay's chest. I pinch one of his peaked nipples between my thumb and forefinger, and he gasps, writhing under my touch, and his pulse jackhammers. I give the same treatment to the other and watch as his hard cock flexes, and a drop of pre-cum drips onto his abs.

My own cock throbs at the sight.

I drag my hand off his throat, slowly down his body, and then wrap it around his cock. I've never touched a dick that wasn't my own, and it feels the same yet oddly different. It's scorching hot in my fist, and the skin is as smooth as the silky ropes around Clay's arms and legs. I can feel his blood pulsing in the thick veins that wrap around his length, and I can imagine the aching pleasure of each pulse.

I give a slow, experimental tug from base to tip, and Clay's head falls back with a deep moan. His hips twitch, but thanks to the bindings, he can't move much more than that. He squirms against the ropes and then moans again.

My own underwear is growing sticky with pre-cum as I stroke Clay and continue to play with and pinch his nipples one and then the other in equal measure.

I pull my hand off his chest long enough to unzip my pants and shove them—along with my underwear—down my thighs.

I cover Clay's body with mine and line my cock up against his. I let out a gasping moan at the sensation. I wrap my hand around both our cocks and thrust against his.

"Oh Jesus," I groan.

I cover his mouth with mine and hump into my tight fist, against Clay's cock.

"Max, oh fuck, oh god."

Clay's cries spur me on, jerking us faster and kissing him deeper until I feel him grow even stiffer against me. Then he lets out a strangled moan, and his cock pulses in my fist. I keep stroking him through his orgasm, his cum coating my fist and my own cock.

My balls draw up, and I bite down on Clay's bottom lip as my own pleasure thunders through me.

My cum spurts all over Clay's stomach and chest as he twitches with aftershocks. I pump myself until my balls are empty and I have thoroughly marked Clay.

When I'm spent, I collapse beside him.

It takes a few minutes for my breathing to return to normal, and when it does, I notice Clay squirming a bit, still bound to the frame.

"Oh my god, I'm so sorry." I hurry to untie him.

Once he's released, he rolls onto his side, facing me with the most content expression I've ever seen him wear.

"You look so beautiful like this. You're practically glowing."

"Mm," Clay hums and smiles. "My ex, Jake, he always said I was like Christmas lights; I get so tied up in knots, I need to be unraveled so I can shine."

"That's cheesy but kind of beautiful," I chuckle, laying down beside Clay and pulling him into my arms.

He tenses for a second before relaxing into my arms.

"Did I do everything right?" I ask, feeling

suddenly insecure.

"It was perfect," Clay sighs and nuzzles closer, pressing his nose and then his lips to the base of my throat.

Maybe it should feel strange holding a man in my arms, but it certainly doesn't feel any stranger than kissing and jerking him off.

"Are *you* okay with everything?" Clay checks.

"Yeah," I assure him. "Better than I ever would've expected, actually. This feels...*right*."

Clay is quiet for much longer than I expect, and I start to wonder if he's fallen asleep, when he finally speaks again.

"This is what you need right now, and it's what I need, too. Let's leave it at that."

I open my mouth to protest, but when I look down, there's a pleading in his eyes that stops me in my tracks.

"You are *not* a phase, or an experiment, or whatever else you're thinking right now." Clay gives me a sad smile and then tucks his face back against my chest. "By the way, I'm going to borrow one of your ropes to practice with, so I can learn to do it right for you."

"You're already doing it right, love."

"I can do it better. I want to practice some knots and get used to the feel, so I can learn more complicated patterns."

"You're perfect," Clay sighs, and I kiss the top of his head.

I'm not perfect, but I want to be for Clay.

CHAPTER 14

Clay

My body feels like it's made of squishy marshmallows, and my brain is pleasantly quiet when I wake up. I wiggle against the large body spooned around me and let out a happy sigh.

I don't know what's going on with Max, but last night was unbelievable.

My dick shifts against my stomach, already hard and getting harder at the memory of Max's hands and mouth all over me last night.

I shift and end up with Max's monstrous cock wedged between my ass cheeks.

A sleepy moan vibrates in his chest and makes my balls tingle.

In the past ten years, I've been too focused on finding a man I'm compatible with in bed to worry too much about finding a man who's my type. But Max is all that and then some. He's pure, unfiltered masculine energy. He's all hair, sweat, and rough hands.

And the way he took care of me last night? I shiver at the memory. He was a little unsure of himself at first, but once he got going with binding me, I could tell he liked it as much as I did. Every time he looked at me tied up and spread out for him, he let out a little moan. I'm not even sure he realized he was doing it, but it was hot as fuck.

"Good morning," Max rasps in a sleep rough voice, his lips brushing against the back of my neck.

"Morning," I reply breathlessly.

"What do we have here?" Max asks playfully as he palms my erection through the sheets.

"We generally call that morning wood, big guy."

"You call it morning wood, I call it break-fast."

"Jesus," I whimper, grinding into his hand. "Weren't you straight like five minutes ago?"

"Apparently not so much." Max chuckles as he nibbles my throat.

As much as I want to just leave it at that and enjoy what his hand is now doing, I know I need to make sure he's not feeling weird about anything that's happened.

"Max," I gasp. "Hold on a second."

His hand stills.

"Did I do something wrong?"

"Hell no, you're incredible. I just want to make sure you're okay. I know we were just joking about it, but you *were* straight like five minutes ago."

"I don't think I was though," Max argues. "I think I have been in denial about my attraction to you for a long time."

My breath catches, and I have the urge to pinch myself. This can't be real. God, Beck is going to have so many *I told you sos* ready for me.

"So, do you think you're bi?"

I feel Max shrug against my back.

"I don't know; I guess so. I've been wrestling with it in my head for two weeks, and I don't have an answer. But maybe it doesn't need a label. Once you put a label on something, there are all these expectations. I know I'm really into you. Does there need to be more of an explanation than that?"

"No, that's enough for me. But what does that *mean* for us? Are we dating?" I ask as I run my fingers up and down the arm Max still has wrapped around me.

"Can we take things slow?" he asks with uncertainty in his voice. "I'm not sure I'm ready to be out in the open or whatever. But I *do* want to take you nice places and be able to kiss and touch you whenever I want when we're at home. Is that okay?"

"Yeah, that's okay," I agree with a smile.

"Now, where were we?" He wraps his hand around my flagging erection and starts to stroke again. "The bondage stuff, is that a requirement for sex for you?"

"Yeah, kind of," I admit, bracing myself for that to be a deal breaker. Sure, tying someone up once in a while can be fun, but who wants to be with someone that they *have* to restrain every time?

"Does it have to be ropes, or am I allowed to get creative with restraints? You seemed okay with being held down the other night instead of being tied."

My heart rate ticks up at the memory. "I need to be unable to move. I need to feel like my partner is worrying about all my pleasure, and all I need to do is feel it."

"I can definitely handle that," Max agrees without hesitation.

A wave of relief washes over me, and I nearly cry with relief. Is it possible Max could accept every part of me?

It's been so long since I've been with someone I trust the way I trust Max. In fact, I haven't trusted a partner since Jake left.

I roll to face Max and wrap my hand around his thick shaft for the first time. It's hot and smooth in my hand, hard and begging for my mouth.

"You've had all the fun so far; I think it's my turn."

I shove Max's shoulder and climb on top of him once he's on his back.

I can't resist running my hands all over his broad, furry chest and down his firm abs. I never thought much about hair on a man before, but damn, does it work on Max.

Max's hands on my ass squeeze and massage.

"In case you're wondering, just because I've never been with a man doesn't mean I've never done butt stuff," Max assures me as I kiss along his chest.

I snort a laugh. "*Butt stuff*? Did you really just say butt stuff?"

Max rolls his eyes and smiles at me as I pinch one of his nipples, eliciting a hiss of pleasure.

"I've eaten and fucked ass; is that what you're looking for?" Max corrects.

"Oh, it's definitely what I'm looking for," I tease. "But not right now. This morning I'm going to suck you off and then make you a nice breakfast."

"Careful, you're going to spoil me."

"You deserve to be spoiled." With that, I dip under the blankets and finally get up close and personal with Max's impressive cock.

He's heavy in my hand. And he's uncircumcised. I've never had the opportunity to play with an uncut cock before, and there's something I've always wanted to do...

I lick around the crown and then gently nibble at his foreskin, and Max jackknifes off the bed.

"Holy fucking shit," he gasps, and I grin to myself.

I press a kiss to the base of his shaft and then run my tongue from root to tip like I'm licking a Popsicle.

Max threads his fingers through my hair as he writhes under my teasing ministrations.

After a dozen or so licks, I focus my attention back on the sensitive skin around the head. I suck and nibble it again while Max moans and bucks his hips.

By the time I finally stretch my lips around

him and take his cock into my throat, Max is begging and tugging at my hair in an attempt to speed me up.

It's been ages since I've had a nice, big cock down my throat, and fuck, if I haven't missed it. The weight of it, the musky taste against my tongue. I moan around him as I bob my head up and down, taking him down my throat over and over again.

"Oh Jesus. Fuck, that's good," Max murmurs, his hips twitching and his fingers tightening in my hair.

I put my hands over his and guide him to shove my head, use me however he needs. It takes a few seconds for Max to catch on, but once he does, we both moan.

Max holds my head in place as he fucks my throat. My eyes water and my own cock leaks onto the sheets beneath me. It's not bondage, but fuck if Max taking what he needs from me isn't doing all kinds of things to me.

With one hand, I cup Max's heavy balls, rolling them in my palm and gently tugging. And with my other hand, I jerk my own cock. I rarely jerk off since I can't get off properly without restraint. But Max's deep moans and fat cock in my throat are doing a fantastic job getting me off.

Max slams his hips harder against my face, driving his cock deep into my throat until I can't breathe. But who the fuck needs air when you can have a gorgeous man fuck your throat instead?

Max lets out a guttural moan, and he grows even harder against my tongue. Then he starts to pulse in my throat. I swallow around him and jerk myself faster until globs of sticky cum coat my fingers.

Max

"Jesus you're good at that," I pant as Clay crawls back out from under the sheets with swollen lips and a self-satisfied grin.

"You're fun to play with," he tells me, his voice rough from the treatment I just gave his throat. *Fuck, that's hot.*

I notice his hand covered in cum and his spent cock. "I thought you couldn't get off without being bound?" I ask.

Clay shrugs. "I usually can't, but that was really fucking hot with you fucking my mouth like that."

I wonder for a second time in less than twelve hours if maybe Clay isn't as entirely opposed to dominance as he's said.

Clay reaches for a dirty t-shirt off his floor and uses it to wipe his hand off. Then he grabs a pair of sweatpants and pulls them on.

"Come on, I want to feed you before you have to get to work."

I follow him, making a quick stop in my room to get dressed. Normally, I'd shower, but a glance at the clock tells me there isn't quite enough time unless I want to be late to work.

I make coffee while Clay whips up some scrambled eggs and toast. As we move around the kitchen in perfect harmony, it hits me that we've been living like a married couple for years, it's just taken us this long to get around to the sex part.

I glance over at Clay, and our eyes meet. He gives me a shy smile that makes my heart flutter in my chest. I grab his arm and tug him close for a brief kiss.

"I had no idea you were so handsy," Clay comments with a laugh.

"Are you complaining?" I cock an eyebrow at him.

"Not at all. Feel free to manhandle me anytime you like." Clay presses one more kiss to my lips before turning back to the eggs and scooping them onto two plates.

After breakfast, I wish Clay a nice and day and then rush out the door.

When I get to work, I start to wonder if I should've taken the extra ten minutes to grab a shower this morning. What if my brothers can smell Clay all over me? I'm not even sure a shower would've helped.

"Whoa, somebody finally got laid," Tony shouts the second I walk into the garage.

I cringe and run a hand through my unkempt hair.

"Who was she?" Gio asks with a smirk.

I consider lying all together, but I'm sure there's

no denying what's written all over my face. I got laid, and it was unbelievable. I bite down on my lip to keep from smiling too widely.

"Just...someone," I answer vaguely.

What would my brothers think if they knew the best night of my life was spent with a man? Not to mention the most epic blowjob of all time. Hell, no woman has ever known how to work my dick like that. Don't get me wrong, women are great. But none of them have ever owned me the way Clay did this morning. And maybe that says more about me than about the women I've been with.

"Must've been someone incredible based on that little smirk you've got going on," Tony notes, elbowing Gio.

"Yeah," I agree with a little cough to cover up the emotion clogging my throat.

"You boys going to do any work, or just stand around gossiping like a bunch a ladies all day?" my dad calls out as he enters the garage from his office. It's a rhetorical question, so we all give a sheepish look and make our way to our corners of the garage.

"Max, your mother wanted me to make sure you're bringing Georgia over for a family birthday dinner on Saturday?"

"Yeah Dad. Clay and I are taking her out to the museum for the day; it's okay if I bring him with for dinner, right?"

"Of course. You know how your mother is; she's not happy unless she's feeding an army."

I nod in agreement and try to ignore the ice in my gut. I'm going to have to tell my parents about Jess moving with Gigi. But maybe it can wait until after I talk to Beck again and find out if I really am shit out of luck.

My dad claps me on the shoulder and then lets me get to work on the Caddy I had up on the lift from yesterday.

Clay

"Ooo, someone looks like he's been properly fucked," Beck comments as soon as I enter On Pointe.

"Maybe," I hedge with a smirk.

I forgot how much good a bondage session could do for my anxiety. I'm still feeling fluffy and light like my body is made of clouds. It wasn't as drawn out as I would've liked last night, but for his first time, Max seemed to have an excellent grasp on what he was doing.

Beck chuckles and quirks one of his perfectly shaped eyebrows at me. "Who are you kidding, honey? You're glowing."

"A gentleman doesn't get ravaged by a hunk and tell," I quip.

"No fair, I told you when Gage and I finally got down and dirty," Beck pouts.

"Exactly, you are far from a gentleman."

Beck punches me in the arm, and I laugh as I try to dodge out of the way of a second hit.

"Seriously though, you look happy and that

makes me happy." Beck gives me a quick kiss on the cheek, and I smile at him.

"Thank you. It's been awhile since anything has made me this happy."

"You deserve it."

Max

When I get off work, I have a few hours to kill before Clay gets home. I decide it's the perfect time to do a little research.

I grab my laptop and settle on my bed. Clay's reactions to dominance are at odds with what he told me he needs, and I know I have to gain a better understanding of how to take care of him.

After slogging through a few porn sites that aren't at all helpful in figuring anything out. I finally find a blog by a couple in a D/s relationship.

I read through several posts and come to two major conclusions: First, Clay may only think he doesn't like dominance because he's never had a partner he's trusted before. And second, it's my job to read Clay's body language and give him what I know he needs.

The main thing I've taken away from our previous conversations was that Clay doesn't want humiliation and he doesn't want pain. Maybe he doesn't realize it's possible for me to use some dominance to simply care for him.

The front door opens, and I close my laptop.

"Honey, I'm home," Clay calls out, and I smile.

I *will* give him everything he needs.

CHAPTER 15

Clay

I finish putting the bow on Gigi's present and then put it on the small pile of gifts. Max always lectures me about getting Gigi too many gifts for her birthday; he says she already has enough junk. But he can shove it, because I love spoiling my little pancake monster.

I open my bedroom door and carry the small pile of presents out to the kitchen. Then, I pull out the ingredients and implements for pancakes, so Gigi can help me make them when she gets up. After that, I start coffee and sit down at the table to browse social media until Max and Gigi wake up.

A few minutes later, Max appears in the kitchen barefoot and sleep rumpled. My chest squeezes, and a smile tugs at my lips.

It's been a week since the first time Max kissed me, and he's slept in my bed every night since. But we agreed that with Gigi here this weekend, it would be best if we stayed in our own rooms. Last night, all alone in my bed, was pure torture.

I want to get up and kiss his sexy mouth. Then I'd love for him to drag me to my bedroom, tie me to the bed, and have his way with me. But, I'd settle for just the kiss.

Max's eyes land on the gifts, and he sighs. "How many times to I have to tell you Gigi has too much junk as it is. You didn't have to get her anything."

I roll my eyes at him. "You're insane if you thought I wasn't going to get her anything. I love the little half-toothless smile, and you will not take that joy from me."

Max's expression softens at my words. He opens his arms, and I waste no time scrambling up and going to him. He wraps me in a hug and kisses the top of my head.

"Thank you for loving Gigi so much."

"Psh, you don't have to thank me for that."

"I know, but I'm still thankful." He kisses the top of my head one more time before releasing me at the sound of tiny feet thundering down the hallway.

"It's my birthday!" Gigi shrieks, skidding to a halt in the kitchen.

"I know, I can't believe you're seven years old," Max says, stooping down to hug his daughter.

It's always made me a little melty inside to watch Max with Gigi. But now that we're—*well, whatever we are*—it's making me swoon even more than usual.

Gigi looks over at the pile of presents on the table, and her eyes go wide.

"Can I open them?"

"Sure, sweetie. But do you want to help me make pancakes first or do presents first?"

"Presents," Gigi decides immediately.

Max and I chuckle as she hurries to tear into the colorful wrapping. Despite what Max thinks, I didn't go too overboard. I got her a few books I thought she'd like, a Barbie, and a Hatchimal— whatever the hell that is.

"Thanks, Clay." Gigi throws her arms around my neck and squeezes. I hug her back and kiss her cheek.

"You're welcome. Now, how about those pancakes?"

Gigi bounces out of her seat and starts measuring out the pancake mix while I crack the eggs.

Once everything is in the bowl, I let Gigi stir, and I glance over my shoulder at Max, who's watching me with heat in his eyes.

I raise an eyebrow at him, and he smirks, letting his eyes roam over my ass.

Behave, I mouth at him, and we both chuckle.

"Why are you laughing?" Gigi asks, looking over at me suspiciously.

"Your daddy was making a funny face," I lie, peeking at the batter to make sure there aren't any lumps left. Even though I don't see any, I still give it exactly three more stirs before feeling satisfied to help her pour the batter into the pan and force myself not to glance back at Max again, even though I can feel his eyes all over me.

Instead of giving in, I count the bubbles as they appear in the cooking batter.

After breakfast, Max sets Gigi up in the living room with some Disney movie that she's seen a hundred times, so we can get showered and dressed.

In the bathroom, I strip down and turn on the water to start heating it up.

The door creaks open, and I'm surprised to see Max slipping into the bathroom with a length of my rope in his hands.

I tremble with excitement, my cock hardening instantly.

"What are you doing? Gigi is right out there," I argue weakly, eyeing the rope as he slides it between his fingers suggestively.

"She's singing *Let It Go* at the top of her lungs. We've got ages before she wonders where we are. And all I want to do is share the shower to save some time."

"Somehow I doubt that's *all* you want to do." I smirk as he drops his pants and his thick cock springs free.

"Turn around for me, petal." Max's tone is gruff, but there's a gentle undertone that keeps me from bristling at the command.

I turn and face the shower, my back to Max. Out of the corner of my eye, I can see Max in the mirror, approaching me slowly.

Max's warm breath puffs against the back of my neck as he runs a rough finger from the base of my neck down my spine, making me shiver.

"Put your wrists together," Max whispers in

my ear, and I comply.

He tickles the rope down my back along the same path his finger took.

I squirm and whimper, pressing back against Max's broad frame. My cock stands at full attention, bobbing in front of me.

Max loops the rope around my wrists and secures them. Then he steps back, leaving me cold and aching for him.

I turn my head to look over my shoulder and watch as Max peels his shirt off. My mouth waters at the sight of his gorgeous, bare body. Rippling muscles, thick, dark hair, and his heavy erection swaying between his thighs all have my knees weak.

Max steps around me and pulls back the shower curtain. "Come on, petal."

Max helps me into the shower, and I groan quietly as the hot water hits my skin.

Max's hot lips trail down my neck as he grasps and massages my ass cheeks.

"Mmm, feels so good," I whimper.

"Shh, we don't have time for all that. You're going to let me wash you up, and we're going to do Gigi's birthday. Then, we'll get back to our fun tonight after Gigi is in bed. How does that sound?"

I grumble in protest but when Max starts massaging my scalp with shampoo that smells like him I quiet down and let him have his way with me.

After he works the shampoo into my hair,

Max tilts my head back to let the hot stream of water rinse me clean. Next, he pumps a handful of body wash into his palm and runs it all over the planes of my body. After thoroughly soaping my chest, Max wraps a soapy hand around my erection. I groan and thrust into his hand, but he quickly moves on to my balls and then slides his sudsy hands between my cheeks and over my twitching hole.

"Please, Max," I gasp, swaying toward him.

"Shh, petal. I've got you."

Max tilts my chin up and kisses me so sweetly I could almost cry. And then he pulls back and quickly washes his own hair and body. Once he's clean, he reaches around me to shut off the water.

Even though I'm still hard and steel and aching for release, the buzz in my mind is calmed by the care Max is taking of me. He steps out of the shower and grabs two towels. He wraps one hastily around his waist and the other around my shoulders. He lifts me out of the shower and then dries me off.

Once I'm dry, he tugs the knot loose on my wrists and presses another kiss to my lips.

I sigh into his mouth, wrapping my arms around his neck, and letting him hold me up.

"Did I get it right, petal? I know you said you didn't want any of this outside of sex, and that you don't want any dominance. But I thought, maybe…"

"It was perfect. I think you might know what I need better than I do."

A smile blazes across Max's face.

"I just want to make you happy." He runs a thumb along my bottom lip.

"Daddy?" Gigi calls from the living room. I drop my arms reluctantly and take the rope from him, so he can go see what his daughter needs while I slip into my bedroom to get dressed.

Max

Clay was exactly right about Gigi going nuts for the butterfly exhibit. We followed her around the museum all morning as she flitted from display to display. And when we went in the butterfly dome and she got to see them flying around up close and personal? She was over the moon.

"Good call, petal," I reach for his hand over the center console and give it a little squeeze. I check the rearview mirror and find Gigi completely engrossed in her tablet. I don't want to keep things between me and Clay from her, but I want to find the right time to tell her.

"Anytime, love. I told you, I love to see her smile." We pull up in front of my parents' house, and I reluctantly pull my hand out of Clay's.

"We're here, princess," I tell Gigi who chucks her tablet onto the seat beside her and unbuckles herself.

"Grandma and Grandpa!" Gigi squeals as she

scrambles out of the car.

Inside, Gigi runs to my parents to get all the spoiling a grandkid can hope for. Gio and Tony slap me on the shoulder and then turn to Clay with a smirk.

"Why, if it isn't Twinkle Toes," Tony mocks with a smile.

"Nice to see you again Gear Head," Clay responds with a saccharine smile to Tony and then turns to Gio, "Grease Monkey."

I stifle a laugh and resist the urge to put my arm around Clay's shoulder.

"Look at you, glowing and shit," Gio notes, eyeing me with suspicion. "You still seeing that girl?"

Clay stiffens and then turns that smile on me. "You didn't tell me you'd been seeing a girl," Clay says, his voice dripping with sweetness.

"Sure, I did," I raise my eyebrows at Clay and shoot him a warning look. "It's the one I've been seeing every day this week. The *girl* I'm absolutely crazy about, even if I'm not ready to introduce her to my family."

Clay's phony smile falters, replaced by a look of repentance. "Oh yeah. I'm pretty sure she's crazy about you too."

Gio and Tony look between us curiously.

"Told you he'd been spending too much time with the queer," Tony murmurs to Gio.

Clay tenses, and I'm on Tony in a flash, shoving him against the wall and putting my forearms against his neck.

"I told you not to use that fucking word. What the fuck is your problem, asshole?"

Tony puts his hands up in surrender. "I didn't mean anything by it. He *is* a queer. What am I supposed to call him?"

"You could try calling him by his name, dickhead," I suggest through gritted teeth.

"Boys, no roughhousing," my mom admonishes.

I let Tony go with one last warning glare.

The rest of the evening passes in a pleasant whirl of presents, cake, and laughter. But I can't get Tony's words out of my mind. *He is a queer. What am I supposed to call him?* If things continue with Clay, I'm going to have to tell my family eventually. Is that all I'll be to them then? Their *queer* brother?

CHAPTER 16

Clay

When we get home from Max's parents' house, I can tell Max has a lot on his mind. He's been tense since his fight with his brother, and I don't blame him. All of this is new and probably a little scary for him, and I can't imagine what it would feel like to *know* you won't be accepted if you tell the truth. I almost feel selfish hoping one day we'll be together openly.

"Why don't you go relax while I put Gigi to bed?" I offer.

"Only if you promise to come find me when you're done," Max whispers, letting his hand linger on my hip for a few seconds.

"You've got yourself a deal," I agree before heading down the hall to find Gigi in her bedroom, organizing her stuffed animals on her bed. "Ready for a bedtime story, sweetie?"

"Yeah," Gigi agrees with a smile.

"Did you have a good birthday?" I ask as I settle onto the bed next to her.

"Uh-huh. It was really fun." Gigi snuggles into my side as I reach for *Harry Potter and the Sorcerer's Stone* so we can pick up where we left off last time.

"Clay?"

"Yeah, sweetie?"

"Are you coming to New York, too?"

My stomach plummets. "No sweetie, I'm not. Only your mom and Mark are going to New York. Your daddy really wants you to stay with us, but there's a lot of complicated grown up stuff to work out."

"I don't want to leave you, but I don't want to leave my mom either. I want us all to stay together."

"Me too, sweetie." I kiss the top of her head and then open the book and start to read.

I make it through two chapters before Gigi is snoring. I quietly slip out of her room with just one lingering glance. I don't know what Max is going to do with Gigi across the country. I don't know what I'll do either.

I make sure the nightlight in the hallway is on and leave her door open a crack before sneaking into Max's bedroom.

I'm not entirely surprised to find that Max has brought my ropes in here. But I'm certainly intrigued by the kitchen chair that's sitting in the middle of his room.

"What do we have here?" I ask with a curious smile.

Max scoots off his bed and comes toward me with hot intent in his expression. When he reaches me, he tugs me into his arms and buries his nose against my neck.

"I'm sorry my brothers are such assholes," Max

murmurs against my skin, nibbling along the tendons in my throat.

"Shh, it's okay, love. I'm not worried about them; I'm just worried about you."

Max sucks hard on my skin and I gasp, pressing myself more firmly against him.

"Strip and sit in the chair, petal," Max requests authoritatively.

My heart leaps into my throat, and all I can do is nod and follow the instructions.

I leave my clothes in a messy heap near the foot of Max's bed, and then I have a seat on the chair. I jump a little when my bare ass hits the cool wood, but when Max approaches from behind and runs his hands along my chest, tweaking each nipple, and then down my stomach, I shiver for an entirely different reason.

"Arms around the back of the chair, please," Max instructs in a gruff tone, again leaving no room for protest.

I bring my arms together around the back of the chair, my heart already thumping wildly in my chest.

Max binds my wrists much like he did this morning in the shower. But this time, he doesn't leave it at that. He wraps the rope around my torso and then pulls it around the back again to twine through my arms. He moves painstakingly slow as he binds my upper body to the chair.

My chest rises and falls rapidly, my mind going so beautifully blank as Max works.

"Rope drunk," Max murmurs as he comes around the front and runs the back of his hand along my cheek. "That's what some of the instruction sites call this state. You're so beautiful like this, petal."

I watch through hooded lids as Max kneels before me and binds each of my legs to the chair as well with the same meticulous care that he bound my upper body.

I squirm in anticipation. My cock throbs in desperation, my balls already aching and heavy.

Max finishes binding my ankles to the legs of the chair, and I can feel all the tension float away as my mind goes quiet. I don't have to worry or obsess about anything. All I have to do is feel whatever Max decides to do to my body.

Max licks his lips and gazes at my cock from his spot on his knees between my legs as a pearl of pre-cum appears at the tip. I've always thought Max was the most gorgeous man alive, but now that I've seen him preparing to suck me off, he's reached a new level of sexy I never knew existed.

My eyes are locked on his lips, inches from my leaking cock.

I'm drunk on thoughts of him sucking me. I need his lips stretched around my shaft as his head bobs up and down my length. Will he get over excited and rush to finish? Or will he torture me with pleasure, edging me for hours with his lips and tongue until I'm crying for relief. A small shiver overtakes me, and fuck me, if I don't hope he goes for option two.

Max wraps his hand around the base of my erection, tentatively at first but growing more confident as he strokes me, dragging his hand slowly from root to tip and back again.

I tilt my head back and close my eyes, giving myself over to him. I know Max would never hurt me or push past my boundaries. I trust Max with my life and my body, completely.

The room is filled with the sound of my panting breath and the steady rhythm of Max's hand on me. I can smell and taste him in the air all around me, and there's a simmering heat in the pit of my stomach.

Then I feel the first tentative lick against the head of my cock, and stars burst behind my eyelids.

"Mmm...that tastes different than I expected," Max muses as he takes another lick like he's trying a new flavor of ice cream.

A sense of awe fills my chest and escapes in a quiet sob. This is the first time Max is touching a man this way.

The heat of his mouth engulfs me, and I let out a strangled whimper. Without any hesitation, Max takes me half way in and wraps his hand around the base, stroking me in time each bob of his head. My head snaps up, I need to see how hot Max looks with my cock between his lips. That's a mental image I'll need in my spank bank for eternity.

My breath catches at the sight. Max's long hair spilling loose and wild over his shoulders, his eyes half lidded, and my glistening cock sliding in and out of his puffy lips.

"Holy fuck," I grind out between my teeth, willing myself not to come yet, not let it end so quickly.

Max slows his pace and pulls off, looking up at me with affection and openness.

"Don't come yet," he says, but it comes out more as a question than a demand.

I whimper and clench my jaw.

"Look at you, so sexy and desperate for me," Max praises, running his hands up my stomach and pinching my nipples before licking around the head of my cock again. "I was a little nervous to taste your cock. I didn't know if it would freak me out to have a dick in my mouth. But god, you taste so good. I love the way I can feel you grow harder against my tongue, and the salty taste of your skin. And, those sounds you're making are driving me crazy. I think I could happily spend the rest of my life right here on my knees for you."

A sob of delight rips from my chest, and I squirm again, wanting so badly to feel Max's hot mouth around me, making me come.

Mercifully, he wraps his lips around me again and returns to the same maddeningly slow sucking that's not likely to make me come anytime soon. My head falls forward as I get lost in the sensations lighting my body on fire. The soft ropes rub against my bare skin nearly everywhere, sending jolts of pleasure through me. My balls throb as Max takes his time with my cock in his mouth.

I lose track of time as my mind settles into the calm place. It feels like Max brings me to the brink at least a dozen times before slowing down and pulling me back.

Saliva drips down my cock and pools around my ass, making my hole twitch to be filled.

My entire body is like one giant, pulsing orgasm waiting to happen as Max picks up speed, taking me as deep as he can and using his hand to help.

This time as the heat rises in the pit of my stomach and my balls draw up tight, he doesn't slow his pace. I bite my lip against the moans that threaten to escape.

"Please Max, I'm so close," I whimper. My toes curl into the carpet and my body trembles with the force of pleasure that rips through me. "Oh god, Max."

He doesn't pull off, sucking me through the earth-shattering orgasm and taking all my cum down his throat without complaint.

I slump against the chair, drained and satisfied beyond anything I've experienced before.

Max stands and unzips his pants, pulling out his flushed, throbbing erection and jerks himself forcefully. Each one of his grunts and groans sends a shot of pleasure to my already spent dick. And then he tenses, and shot after shot of thick cum hit my chest and stomach. I close my eyes and revel in the feeling of being marked by Max—claimed, owned.

I barely notice as he unties me and carries me to

his bed. I feel the rough fabric of a towel against my skin, cleaning Max's release off me. And then the bed shifts as he climbs in beside me and sleep pulls me under.

Max

"Daddy, are you and Clay having a sleep-over?" Gigi's whisper startles me awake. I clutch for the bed sheet and pull it up so she doesn't see anything.

"Uh, yeah, princess," I answer quickly. "Why don't you go to the kitchen, and I'll be right out to make you breakfast?"

Gigi shrugs and skips out of my bedroom.

I glance over at Clay, still fast asleep beside me and looking breathtakingly peaceful. I smile at the memory of last night. I never thought I could enjoy going down on another man, but that was hot as hell. I guess I shouldn't be that surprised; I've always enjoyed pleasuring my partners, even above myself. And having a dick in my mouth wasn't nearly as strange as I expected it to be. After all, when you think about it, all genitals in your mouth are strange as it is.

I brush a kiss to Clay's cheek and climb out of bed. I grab a pair of sweatpants out of my dresser, tug on a t-shirt, and then go to find Gigi.

I find her in the kitchen dancing around with one of her bunny stuffed animals. I slide into a chair and smile at the missing one at the other end of the table.

"Can I talk to you for a second, princess?" I ask, patting the seat of the chair beside me.

I may not be ready to tell the world. But there's no reason not to talk to Gigi about what's going on with Clay and me.

"Sweetie, you know how your mom and Mark hold hands and kiss, and they want to be together forever?" Gigi nods and ties her bunny's ears in knots and then unties them. "How would you feel if Clay and I were like that, too?"

"You love Clay?" Gigi asks.

"There are a lot of ways to love someone. And I do love Clay as a friend, and maybe soon I'll love him as more than a friend." I don't know why I'm giving a child such a complicated explanation, but she just nods again like it makes complete sense to her.

"So, I'd have three daddies and a mommy?"

"Maybe someday. Would that be okay?"

"Clay is fun. I like him," Gigi declares. "Can we have pancakes for breakfast?"

I chuckle. If only everyone could see things as simply as a child. "Sure, sweetie."

I fumble through helping Gigi make pancakes, not quite as practiced at it as Clay is. But we manage not to burn them, so I'm calling that a win.

Clay enters the kitchen still dressed in his pajamas with a big yawn. With the newfound freedom of my confession to Gigi, I step forward and pull my man into a quick kiss.

He stumbles but smiles and then casts a curious

look from me to Gigi.

"My daddy wants to kiss you and be with you forever," Gigi declares with a smile.

"*Forever?*" Clay coughs, his eyes going wide.

"Relax petal, it was a hypothetical. What I was explaining to Gigi is that you and I are together like Jess is with Mark."

"Oh," Clay relaxes and smiles at Gigi. "Are you happy about that, sweetie?"

Gigi shrugs. "I think kissing is gross."

"Good, you don't need to be kissing anybody for at least twenty years."

Clay laughs and goes to grab the maple syrup out of the fridge.

I go to grab the extra chair out of my bedroom, so Clay has somewhere to sit.

Once we're all seated and digging into breakfast, my mind wanders back to Gigi's question earlier. I watch Clay as he makes Gigi laugh, and my heart swells.

For five years, Clay has been the person I've leaned on, looked forward to spending time with the most, and always sought to share both my happiness and failures with. I don't know how it possibly took me this long to see how in love with him I am.

Clay glances over at me and cocks his head. "Why are you looking at me like that?"

"How am I looking at you, petal?"

"Like a weirdo. Stop it; you're creeping me out," he demands and we both laugh.

Yeah, there's no doubt I'm head over heels for this man.

CHAPTER 17

Clay

I'm sitting behind my desk chewing my nails bloody when Beck walks in.

"Gross, knock that off," he chides, swatting my hand out of my mouth.

"Excuse me, I have a lot on my mind," I snap.

"What's wrong? Are things still going well with Max?"

"Max is perfect," I sigh. "That's the problem."

"Sweetie, that makes no sense."

"Beck, what's the next step with all this stuff with Jess and Gigi?"

Beck sighs and gives me a pitying look. "He can take her to arbitration to try to get primary custody. That's pretty much his last chance to make anything happen. Technically, he could appeal to a judge, but I don't see it making a huge difference if arbitration doesn't go his way."

"That's what I figured. I think he should move out to New York so she doesn't lose him in her life."

Beck puts a hand over mine. "You'll just let him go like that?"

I shrug, forcing my face to stay neutral as my heart fractures. "What choice will I have?"

"Sweetie, you could—"

"No, I couldn't," I cut Beck off. "Let's just see what happens, I guess."

Max

Beck is waiting for me at the coffee shop just like we discussed. He's sipping a coffee and looking down at his phone with a smile. I have no doubt he's texting with Gage. I've known Beck for several years, and I've never seen him light up over anyone the way he does with Gage.

I order a drink and join Beck at his table.

"Hey, so did you talk to Jess about mediation?" Beck asks as soon as I sit down.

"Yeah, she's not going for it. She said it won't change anything. Level with me, is there any chance of me getting custody if I take Jess to arbitration?"

Beck tilts his head back and forth as if to say *so-so*. "I'd put your odds at *maybe* fifty percent. There's no reason *not* to grant you custody, but the fact is most of the time the mother is favored. You can certainly try to argue that Gigi is already established at school here and that it would be wrong to uproot her."

"I have to try."

Beck nods in understanding.

"I'll request arbitration if this is what you want. I just don't want you to get your hopes up too high, okay?"

"Yeah, I understand."

I'm strung tighter than a guitar string about to snap. Even the ride home with my bike rumbling beneath me didn't do anything to settle me. There's only one thing I can imagine focusing my energy at this point, and it's on the other side of this door.

I take a deep breath to try to get myself under control enough to go in there without scaring Clay.

When I step inside, Clay is exactly where I imagined he would be, sprawled out on the couch, drumming his fingers on the coffee table and swinging one foot as it dangles over the arm of the couch.

"Hey," he greets me with a smile.

I slip my shoes off and stalk toward him, feeling my muscles unknot with every step in his direction.

When I reach him, I crook my finger at him to get him to stand, adding a puppy dog look so he knows it's a request and not a demand.

Clay hesitates for a second before getting up and looking up at me through his eyelashes.

"Can I help you with something, sweetie?" Clay asks with a teasing lilt.

I wrap my arms around his waist and pull Clay against me, burying my nose in the crook of his neck and taking a deep inhale.

"Can I play with you?" I rumble against the side of his neck, nibbling along the sensitive tendon.

Clay whimpers and nods. "Do you want to go to my room?" he asks in a shaky voice.

"I want you to strip and go get your ropes. And then I want to tie you up and keep you here on the couch with me the rest of the night where I'll tease you and play with you for hours while we watch a movie."

Clay gasps, and the tent in the front of his pants grows more prominent.

"Yes," he whispers, his hands fisting the front of my shirt as if my words made him weak in the knees.

My hands around his waist sneak up the back of his shirt, and my fingers memorize the feel of his smooth skin. My lips press to his neck, his jaw, his chin, and finally hard against his mouth.

Our hands work together now to rid him of his shirt, our kiss parting just long enough to fling his shirt away. His pants are next, left in a pile at his feet.

I swallow Clay's whimpers and panting breaths as I grasp and massage the round, firm globes of his ass. My cock dribbles pre-cum, leaving my pants sticky and uncomfortable. But I don't want this to end anytime soon. I want to tease Clay—tease myself—until he's sure he'll die if he can't come. I want the pleasure to hit him so hard he can't remember a time when I wasn't giving him everything he ever needed.

"Go get your bindings," I request, and Clay shudders in my arms. "Wait, I have a better idea; I'll go get your bindings."

"You want me to wait here?"

"You want to know what I *really* want?" I ask, a little afraid of scaring him if I admit the truth.

Clay hesitates, his body shifting away from me like he's contemplating bolting. After a few breaths, he relaxes in my arms.

"Yes," he breathes like he's admitting something he hadn't planned to.

"I want you to get on the couch, on your knees, facing the wall. I want you to grab your elbows and wait for me to come bind you so beautifully so that we can both be unraveled.

Clay lets out a shuddering breath and gazes up at me through his eyelashes. I can see the war behind his eyes between his desire to give control over to me and his fear of being dominated and controlled. I run the back of my hand down his cheek and then cup his jaw and trace my thumb along his bottom lip.

"I will *never* do anything to break your trust. I only want to take care of you and give us both what we need." Even if I haven't known about this craving inside myself as long as Clay has, I can't deny it's something I desperately need. Binding Clay and being the sole person responsible for his pleasure and needs, there's a headiness about that I've never known until now.

Clay's Adam's apple bobs as he swallows, and then he gives a barely perceptible nod and kisses my thumb, which is still resting on his bottom lip.

"I believe you."

Then he turns and gets on the couch exactly as I'd requested—facing the wall, on his knees, grabbing his elbows.

I step up behind him and trace my finger down his spine. I nibble on his neck and smile when he shivers.

"Wait right here for me, petal. I'll be right back."

Clay nods.

I head straight for his room to grab his ropes, my cock aching in the confines of my jeans. When I return to the living room, Clay is exactly as I left him and that sets something primitive in my chest howling in approval.

I step up behind him and ghost my lips along the back of his neck while I start to work the rope around his hands and then around his torso.

This time, I take my time, trying to create a diamond design like I've seen on several videos. It didn't seem like a difficult design, so I thought it would be an easy one to start with. The time and concentration it requires to get the design right is enough to get my mind off everything else and bring me solidly into the moment.

Clay pants and whimpers as I work but doesn't try to hurry me or complain. His muscles twitch and tremor under my touch.

"Mmm, so sexy," I murmur against his ear. "Can I take a picture of you?"

Clay hesitates before nodding. I reach into my pocket and snap a picture of Clay's arms bound behind his back with the diamond shaped design in the rope.

My mind wanders back to a few weeks ago when I first found the picture of Clay bound and beautiful. I can't believe it was such a short time ago. It feels like that was a different lifetime. In a way, I think it was.

"I found a picture of you," I admit as I run my finger along the exposed skin between the ropes. "It was on your floor, and I took it. I'm sorry, I couldn't help myself."

"When?" Clay asks breathlessly.

"A few weeks ago. I couldn't take my eyes off how sexy you looked. I knew I shouldn't take it, but I was mesmerized by you."

"I don't mind. Hell, if I'd have known that was what it would take to finally have you, I'd have given you the picture myself."

"I think you've had me for longer than either of us realized, petal."

After I take a few photos on my phone, I position Clay onto his stomach on the couch and pull his legs up to bind them to his arms.

By the time I'm finished, Clay is panting, and his skin is flushed from head to toe. I roll him onto his side, so he'll be more comfortable, and then I take a moment to admire my handiwork.

My cock aches as I look down on Clay completely mine to touch and play with. I unzip my pants and pull my heavy erection out, giving myself a slow stroke as my eyes roam over the blissful expression on Clay's face and the way his cock pulses and twitches, desperate for my touch.

Clay

A dribble of pre-cum slides from the tip of my cock and down the length toward my balls. And I'm so sensitive I can feel the entire journey like a caress. I squirm for a moment and feel the tether of my bindings holding me in place, and a wave of perfect bliss washes over me and quiets all the thoughts in my head.

"You're so sexy like this, tied up in a neat little bow for me. You're like the best toy I never thought to ask for."

Heat races through me at his words. There's the familiar dominance that usually makes me clench my teeth, but this isn't malicious or controlling. Max feels possessive of me...and I like it.

I nod in agreement and let out a contented sigh.

Max's hand wraps around the base of my cock, and he gives me one tortuously slow stroke. I gasp when he reaches the head and runs his thumb through the pre-cum pooling there.

Then, he trails his damp thumb back down my length and over my balls before spreading the sticky pre-cum around my hole.

"Oh Jesus," I gasp, bucking and once again reaching the confines of my bindings. A hot pulse starts in my core and spreads through my limbs.

"You know, I've been wondering what it would be like to shove my tongue in your ass." The deep gravel in Max's tone is the only thing that gives away his otherwise conversational remark.

I wait for him to go on, and when he doesn't, I try to shake the lust from my mind and study his expression. He's given me everything I crave, and now, he needs something from me. Who am I to deny him that?

"It looks to me like I'm at your mercy. Which means you can shove anything in my ass you want."

Max's lips part on a quiet moan, and the flash of heat in his eyes tells me I guessed exactly right. He doesn't want to dominate or control me, but maybe a little bit of submission on my part is what does it for him, and maybe giving in to that with someone I trust is what I need, too.

Max's hand continues to tease and caress my skin. He grasps and massages my ass cheek. The air hits my hole as he parts my cheeks, and I shiver. I want his hot tongue on me, his rough fingers inside me, his big cock stretching me open.

"Please," I whine.

"Patience, petal."

Max lifts his hand to my face and runs it along my jaw and then traces my bottom lip with his index finger.

"Open up," he requests, his finger pressed against my mouth.

I open for him, licking and sucking his finger until

it's dripping with my saliva. He pulls it out of my mouth and trails it between my cheeks, teasing it over my hole.

My eyes fall closed, and I bite down on my bottom lip as I give over to the beautifully helpless feeling of being entirely at Max's mercy. He can play with me all night or make me come in two minutes; it's entirely his decision.

"That's right; relax and let me take care of you."

Max's finger circles my hole, increasing the pressure as I soften under his touch. It's been so long since anyone has been inside me; I'm sure I'll lose my mind if Max keeps up his leisurely pace.

Finally, he pushes inside me. Just one teasing finger sliding inside my tight channel. My balls are full and heavy, and my cock is leaking as the rough pad of Max's finger presses into my prostate.

My body fills with blissful peace as Max drives me to the brink and then pulls me back.

A second finger eases in and he sits up on his knees, eyes trained greedily on my expression as he opens me.

"I've been dreaming of tasting your ass," he murmurs as he leans forward and kisses along my thigh, toward my ass.

I close my eyes again and just feel as his tongue teases along my heated skin and then traces my rim while his fingers continue to fuck me.

"So good," I gasp, my cock spasming for contact. Any friction at all would do.

A third finger joins, and I moan.

Max's tongue continues to lick around my hole while his fingers ready me to take his cock. A small voice in the back of my mind wants me to beg him to hurry up and fuck me already. But a much larger part of my consciousness is too far into a blissful state, completely at peace with Max using me any way he wants.

"You're so tight. I need to feel you wrapped around me. Please tell me I can make you mine."

"Yes," I gasp.

"Oh shit, I need lube and stuff. Don't move." Max winks, and I whimper when his fingers slip out of me.

I hear his heavy footfalls as he jogs down the hallway to his bedroom and then as he returns seconds later.

I watch through heavy eyelids as he rolls the condom on with practiced motions and then squirts a generous amount of lube into his hand. He coats his cock, and I shiver as he smears the remainder into my crease and around my hole.

"Are you ready for me, petal?"

I nod frantically. I've never been more ready for anything in my life.

Max rolls me onto my stomach, and then the head of his cock presses against my entrance.

Max's lips trail along my shoulders as he eases into me so gently it steals my breath. His hands roam over my body, once again tracing the areas of skin that peek out between the ropes.

By the time his hips are flush against my ass

cheeks, I'm burning with the need to be rode hard and fast.

If I had the leverage, I'd push back and force him to take me the way I'm craving. But as it is, I'm at his mercy. And I fucking love it.

"I've got you, petal," Max assures me as if he can read my mind.

He pulls out and then slams back into me with enough force to rattle my teeth, and I cry out joyfully. He does it again, and I'm already seeing stars. My cock grinds into the soft cushion of the couch beneath me as he fucks into me fast and deep.

He sits back on his knees and grabs my bound legs and uses them as leverage to take me rougher still. With the new angle, he pegs my prostate with every thrust and in no time, I'm a panting, babbling wreck.

"Oh god, Max. I'm...oh fuck," I wail as my body lights with pleasure, my ass clenching hard around his cock as it continues to ram me.

Max grunts and fucks harder until I feel his body stiffen, and he swells inside me and then pulses out his own release.

He pants and gives a few weaker thrusts before he slips out. The sudden absence of him inside me, filling me, leaves me feeling empty and cold. But the rest of my body feels like it's floating away on marshmallow clouds.

I'm vaguely aware of a gentle tugging as Max unties me, but I can't be bothered to move or open my eyes. After a few minutes, Max picks me up and tucks me against his chest.

"Why don't we go lay down and take a nap. Then when we wake up, I'll make dinner and we can watch a movie together."

I nod and sigh with contentment as I curl my body against him.

CHAPTER 18

Max

Beck greets me with a smile when I walk through the door of Clay's dance studio.

"Hey, what brings you by tonight?" Beck asks, cocking his head to one side. I suppose it is rare for me to stop by On Pointe, but not unheard of by any means.

"I was just sitting at home missing my—Clay." I feel my cheeks heating at my slip up.

I glance over and catch sight of Clay through the door to one of the dance studios. He's in front of a class demonstrating a dance move. I can't take my eyes off him, the peace and joy on his face is so beautiful. His body is fluid as he spins with a flourish. My heart stutters as I find myself leaning against the doorway, unable to turn away.

"You've got it bad, don't you?" Beck says from behind me.

My cheeks burn hotter. "I...uh...it's not..."

"No need to blush, stud. Clay has already told me *all* the details, and you don't have anything to be shy about." Beck winks at me.

"Everything?"

"He's lying," Clay calls from inside the studio, and Beck laughs.

"Fine, he hasn't told me *everything*," Beck concedes. He casts a quick look toward Clay who's back to explaining something to his students. Beck moves closer to me and drops his voice. "I've never seen him as happy as he's been the past few weeks. Don't hurt him. I know it's early on and sometimes things don't work out, but please be kind to him if things end."

"I'd never hurt him. I would've thought you'd know that by now."

Beck nods once with satisfaction, and I get back to creeping on Clay while he finishes his class.

Clay

I force myself to keep my attention on my class. But I can't help sneaking a few glances at Max as he stands in the doorway, watching me with a small smile on his lips. My stomach flutters, and I smile back.

"Is that your boyfriend?" Amelia—the youngest student in my advanced class—asks, peeking over her shoulder at Max.

"Uh...yeah," I admit, feeling a blush creeping up my neck.

"He's really hot."

"You don't have to tell me," I agree with a laugh.

Twenty minutes later, my class wraps up, and I finally make my way over to Max, so I can find out what brought him by. Not that I'm complaining.

"Hey, petal," Max greets when I reach him. The endearment is quiet enough I'm sure only I can hear. I almost offer my lips for a quick kiss before I realize we're in public, and Max isn't ready for any kind of PDA. It's understandable. After all, he's still coming to terms with this whole new side of himself and we've only been together a few weeks.

"What are you doing here?" I ask curiously. "Is everything okay?"

"Yeah, I was thinking I'd take you out once you're finished for the day? It's kind of lame, but I packed a picnic, and I wanted to take you on a ride somewhere."

My mouth falls open. "That's the sweetest thing I've ever heard."

"Sorry, is it totally lame? I'm still getting used to the idea of dating another dude. I know girls eat romantic shit like that up, but maybe I need to plan something more masculine or something for us?"

I laugh and shake my head. "No, love. I like *romantic shit*. And dating a guy isn't so different," I point out.

"No, I guess it's not," Max agrees. Something passes behind his eyes, and he sways toward me like he might kiss me in public after all. But then he straightens up and looks around. "How many more classes do you have today?"

"That was my last one, so I'm good to go."

Max jerks his head toward the door, and I follow him.

"You taking off?" Beck asks.

"Yup. You don't mind locking up after your last class, do you?"

"Of course not, go have fun." Beck waves me off, and I'm more than happy to comply.

Outside, Max offers me a helmet and leather jacket he has slung over the back of his bike, and I take them. My hands shake a little as I prepare to get on the back of the motorcycle for a second time. The first time wasn't as bad as I'd expected. But each time there's a whole new opportunity to become roadkill. Max has been itching to get me back on his bike, but he's been careful not to push.

"Relax, Petal. I won't let anything happen to you."

"*You* won't. What about all the other crazy drivers on the road?"

"You worry too much," Max accuses.

"Yeah, hi, I'm Clay, and I stress about shit, nice to meet you," I deadpan.

"I don't mind, that just means I get to help you *de*-stress later." Max waggles his eyebrows, and I chuckle.

"You're too charming for your own good." I shake my head and then climb onto the bike behind Max with all the grace of a drunk hippo.

Once I'm on and clutching Max around the middle for dear life, the motorcycle roars to life beneath us, and I bury my face in his back, so I don't have to witness the horror of going sixty miles per hour without two tons of metal to protect me.

Max

The feel of Clay clinging to me from behind—his hot breath tickling my back as he hides his face there—makes the ride even more enjoyable than it would normally be. I love the feeling of flying down the open road with the wind on my skin and my bike thundering between my legs. But with Clay plastered against me, the whole experience takes on a whole new level of enjoyment.

"Open your eyes and enjoy the view, petal," I encourage as we get into the mountains.

I feel Clay slowly turn his head, so he's still pressed against me, but I'm assuming he can now look around a little.

"Where are we going?" he calls over the sound of the wind.

"An overlook. It's not much farther."

A few minutes later, I pull into a gravel parking area.

Clay lets go and flexes his fingers.

"A little numb from holding on so tight?" I ask.

"Shut up; that was your plan the whole time. You like that I'm terrified of your motorcycle, so you can get me to hang all over you," Clay complains.

I swing my leg over and then turn to look at him. I tilt his chin up and run my thumb along his bottom lip.

"You and I both know I don't need to scare you to get you close. And I would never stress you out on purpose. I hope you'll like riding with me eventu-

ally. I'd love to do a road trip on the bike sometime together."

Clay's eyes light a little. "Where would we go?"

"Wherever you want." I shrug. "We could head
down the coast and hit some beaches. Or, we
could ride up to Canada and go camping."

"That sounds fun."

"You'll have to get use to her then." I wink and run
my hand along the body of my bike. I grab the trail
bag off the back of my bike and take Clay's hand.

We find a spot with flat ground and a good view,
and then I set down the bag and pull out a small
blanket I packed, followed by some sandwiches
and chips.

"It's nothing fancy," I apologize.

"It's perfect."

"I got the arbitration date today for the custody hearing," I tell Clay after a few minutes of eating and enjoying the view.

Clay swallows the bite in his mouth and
looks at me with worry. "When is it?"

"In two weeks. I'm nervous," I admit. "Beck
doesn't seem confident I can win this."

Clay puts a hand on my knee and then rubs it
up and down my thigh in a comforting motion.

"I know; I'm sorry. If you don't get custody,
we'll have to figure something out."

"Figure what out? That's it, that's the end of
the line," I argue.

Clay frowns and then turns to look out over
the city sitting far beneath us in the distance.

"We'll cross that bridge when we get to it," Clay says ominously.

"Clay—"

"Let's drop this for now and wait to see what happens."

"Yeah, okay," I agree reluctantly. I don't like the look in Clay's eyes, and I don't like the implication. But he's right; there's no need to have this conversation before we know what's going to happen.

CHAPTER 19

Max

I roll over, put my arms around Clay's waist, and then pull him against my chest. He murmurs in his sleep as I nuzzle the back of his neck. I inhale deeply and let his scent calm my racing heart.

Today is the day, and I don't know what I'm going to do if things don't go my way. Beck has made it abundantly clear that this is a total shot in the dark. But I had to at least try. I couldn't let Jess take my kid three thousand miles away without at least trying to get custody.

"You're tense, love," Clay murmurs in his sleep.

"Sorry." I kiss his shoulder and then scoot away and swing my legs over the side of the bed. "Go back to sleep, I'm going to get up and take a shower."

Clay rolls onto his back and yawns widely before eyeing me with concern.

"You want me to come shower with you?" he offers.

"I need a little space to get my head on straight this morning. Thank you though."

"Anything you need, love." Clay throws the blankets off, but I'm too distracted this morning to even enjoy the view of his gorgeous, bare body. "I'll make you breakfast."

"Thank you."

In the bathroom, I crank the water as hot as it will go and then climb into the shower.

My mind swirls, and my hands shake as I let the water cascade over me, wishing it could wash all the fear away.

Once I'm dry and dressed, I head to the kitchen to find that Clay has laid out a veggie omelet and some toast with jam for me.

"You didn't have to do all this."

"Oh hush. Sit down and have something to eat while I get showered and dressed."

I do as he says, mostly because I'm feeling too lost and jittery to consider any sort of disagreement. I feel like I have a date with an executioner today.

My heart is pounding out of my chest as Jess and I approach the stern looking panel of arbitrators.

"We are here to decide the custody of one minor, Georgia Moretti. Why don't you start, Mr. Moretti and tell me why you think you should retain custody of your daughter," the one in the center prompts.

I swallow and look at Beck. He told me to let him do all the talking today.

"Georgia should remain with her father— Max Moretti— when her mother moves to New

York in a few months time. Georgia is already established at the elementary school here, she has friends, and a routine. A major change like moving across the country would be very stressful for her."

The arbitrator nods and writes something down.

"And you, Ms. Thomas. Why should Georgia remain in your custody?"

Similarly, Jess' lawyer answers for her.

"With my client, Georgia will have two caregivers in the home, access to the best schools in New York, and she'll still get to see her father during her school breaks. Max is a single father, with minimal income. He won't have the same resources to provide for Georgia on a day-to-day basis that my client will."

Frustration and shame wash over me. I want Gigi to have everything in the world, and I want to be able to provide those things for her.

"Mr. Moretti," the judge addresses me. "Who would care for Georgia while you're working?"

"Clay," I answer easily. "He's helped me care for her for the past five years. He's great with her, and she loves him very much."

"Your roommate? That's not exactly a stable care provider," Jess argues. "What if he moves out?"

"He's not my roommate; he's my boyfriend," I grit out.

Jess' mouth falls open, and a weight lifts from my shoulders. I don't want to keep hiding what Clay is to me. He's not some random roommate; I love him. *Holy shit, I'm in love with him.*

The arbitrators exit to confer and we all sit awkwardly quiet and waiting. Almost an hour later, they return and my heart jumps into my throat.

"This was a difficult call to make. We appreciate both sides. But, from everything I've heard, I think the best thing for Georgia will be for her mother to have primary custody."

"No," I gasp, feeling my heart tear in two inside my chest. I can't lose my baby. They can't take her from me.

"I'm sorry, Mr. Moretti. I can tell you love your daughter very much, and I'm sure you're an excellent caregiver. I hate having to make these kinds of decisions, but I have to do what I see as the best interest of the child."

I nod mutely, and Beck puts a comforting hand on my shoulder.

Everything is a blur as we exit the courtroom, and I fight to hold back tears.

"How'd it go?" Clay asks, jumping up from the bench he was waiting on in the main area of the arbitrators.

I shake my head, still afraid to open my mouth and attempt to form words. But Clay understands the gesture easily and wastes no time pulling me into a hug. He rubs circles in the middle of my back as I bury my face in the crook of his neck. I stop fighting the tears, allowing sobs to wrack my body. Clay just holds on tighter and whispers soothing words in my ear.

"Let's get you home, love," Clay suggests after a few minutes.

I nod against his shoulder and let him lead me outside to his car. I vaguely register Beck following behind us.

Clay

My heart breaks for Max as he retreats to his bedroom. The thought of only seeing Gigi a few months out of the year has my heart breaking. I can only imagine how Max must be feeling.

I stand in the living room for a few minutes, feeling overwhelmed and useless. What can I possibly do to make him feel better right now? Short of kidnapping Gigi and keeping her here with us, I'm useless. But, at the very least, I can cook him a nice dinner full of comfort food and pamper him a bit tonight.

I head to the kitchen and set to work making Max's favorite—meatloaf, mashed potatoes, and green beans. And for dessert, I'll make him some chocolate chip cookies from scratch.

I get so lost in cooking over the next hour that I don't even hear Max's bedroom door open again.

"What are you doing, petal?" Max asks, wrapping his arms around me from behind and pressing his lips to the back of my neck.

His voice is a little raw and my heart breaks all over again for him.

"I thought you could use something to eat. And

then, after dinner, I'm going to run you a hot bath and give you a massage and anything else you want. How does that sound?"

"That sounds amazing. Thank you; I don't know what I'd do without you."

"You don't have to thank me; it's what friends are for."

"Boyfriends," Max corrects.

"Really?" I ask, unable to fight a smile. "You don't have to say that just because—"

"I'm saying it because it's true. You're mine, and I'm yours. I told you from the beginning this wasn't an experiment or a *quarter life crisis* as you called it. I needed to wrap my head around all of it and adjust my own view of myself. But you *are* my boyfriend. If you'll have me, that is."

"Of course I will, you big dope. Now, why don't you set the table; dinner is about ready."

Max presses one more kiss to my shoulder and then releases me to do as I asked.

Max

I drag myself out of bed, unsure at first what day it is. I called in sick to the garage last week because I couldn't bear to leave my room, let alone the house.

I rub my eyes and groan as I shuffle for the door.

The smell of bleach and lemon cleaner hit my nose and burn my eyes.

"You're up?" Clay says with surprise, the relief written all over his face.

"Um, yeah sorry…"

"Shh, don't apologize. I was worried, that's all."

That explains the extreme cleanliness of the house. Guilt hits me in the chest, imagining Clay over the past week, scrubbing every inch of the house as his anxiety drives him too crazy to sit still for long.

I reach for Clay and pull him into my arms. "I *am* sorry. I should've handled things better. I shouldn't have left you alone to worry about me like this. I'll make it up to you, petal."

Clay nibbles on my neck and then buries his face there, his breath tickling my skin. "I'm just glad you're up and about. Are you going to go to work today?"

"Uh, yeah." I rub my face again. "I should shower and get going."

"Okay. I'm heading out to work now. If you need anything today, text me."

I nod and tilt Clay's face up, so I can suck his bottom lip between mine and then plant a sweet kiss there.

"I'll see you tonight, petal. Have a good day."

"You too."

I feel like I've just come off a bad bout of the flu. My body is weak and tired, even though I've not gotten out of bed in a week. Being at work feels a bit better. The normalcy of it is centering. But I'm far from okay.

"You break up with your girl or something?" Tony asks as I work wordlessly on an engine rebuild.

"No."

"What's got you so mopey then? You called off all last week, and now, you're walking around here like someone died."

"I don't want to talk about it right now, bro."

"Sounds like girl problems to me," Gio chimes in. I roll my eyes at dumb and dumber. I don't understand how I even share genetics with these two idiots.

"Yeah, well, my world doesn't revolve around tits and ass," I snap.

Gio holds his hands up in surrender, and Tony chuckles.

I'd love to tell them about Clay just to see the look on their faces right now. But I can't find the words. Besides, if I don't tell Ma before the knuckleheads, I'll never hear the end of it.

CHAPTER 20

Max

"Hey, Ma, can I talk to you about something?" I slide into a chair at the kitchen table and watch my mother scurry about the kitchen in a tizzy like usual.

"Of course, you can talk to me about anything."

"Can you sit down for a second?" I ask, fidgeting in my seat.

My mom frowns and stops what she's doing to sit down at the table across from me. She reaches for my hand with concern in her eyes.

"What's the matter, *mio figlio?*"

"Nothing, there's just something I need to tell you, and I'm not sure how you're going to feel about it."

"Just tell me. It can't be that bad," she encourages.

"I met someone. I'm in love."

"This is incredible news! Why do you look so nervous to tell me such joyous news? Tell me, who is she?"

"That's the thing; it's not a *she.* It's Clay."

Her smile falters for a second, and she squeezes my hand. "Maybe you just haven't met the right girl yet," she suggests hopefully.

"No, Ma. I've looked for girls. I dated so many girls

who didn't make me feel a fraction of what I feel for Clay. And when I think of how many years I had Clay right in front of me and didn't realize what I was missing...didn't realize how much happiness I was missing out on..." I shake my head as the reality hits me that I easily could've gone on never really seeing him. I could've gone my whole life without Clay lighting me up from the inside out. "All this time, I thought I needed to look for the right girl, but it turned out I had to realize what I really needed was the right *person* to make me happy. And that person is Clay. I know you love me, Ma, and I need you to see what he means to me."

I hold my breath as I wait for her response. I know my dad and brothers are going to have more of a difficult time adjusting to this new development. But ultimately, my mom rules the roost, and if she accepts me with Clay, they'll *have* to come around eventually.

"All I want is for you to be happy, *mio figlio*."

My shoulders sag in relief, and I wrap my arms around my mom and hug her with all the fierce love and appreciation pounding through me.

"I love you, Ma."

"I love you too. Now, when can I meet this man of yours?"

"You've met Clay a hundred times."

"I haven't met him as your boyfriend. You'll bring him to dinner on Saturday."

"Yes, Ma," I reply obediently. "You'll talk to

dad, Gio, and Tony?"

"You don't want to tell them yourself?"

"I don't think they'll take it well," I admit.

"They love you, too. They'll take it well, or I'll give each one of them a swift kick."

I chuckle as relief floods me. "There's one other thing I have to tell you, Ma."

"Go on," she prompts.

"Jess is getting married, and they're moving to New York. I took her to court to try to get custody of Gigi, but I lost. They're leaving in three weeks."

My mom gasps, putting her hand over her heart. Her grandchildren are her life, so I know she's hurting as much as I am over this news.

"There has to be something you can do."

I shake my head. "I've tried everything, and I'm out of options. I'll get Gigi during school breaks, and the rest of the time she'll be in New York with Jess."

Tears roll down her cheeks. "You have to go with her. She needs you."

"I can't. My whole life is here. Clay is here," I argue.

"God has a plan for this; I know he does," she insists.

"You know I don't believe in that stuff, Ma. This is the hand I was dealt, and I'm just going to have to make the best of it." I stand up and then lean over to give her a hug. "I'll bring Clay over for dinner in a few days, and I'll tell Dad, Gio, and Tony about everything. Love you, Ma."

Clay

My feet are killing me when I get off work. All I can think about is a hot bath and a foot rub. And I'm willing to give Max *anything* in exchange for that foot rub.

Max isn't home yet when I arrive, so I strip off my clothes and head into the bathroom to fill the tub. I'm in the process of adding some bath salts—and there might be a little bit of singing and booty shaking—when the door creaks open, and Max pops his head in.

He whistles as his gaze rakes over my body, and a giggle bubbles from my chest.

"You're just in time. Care to join me?"

"Absolutely." Max tears his clothes off and leaves them piled on the floor. I lick my lips at the miles of gorgeous, toned muscle now on display.

Max climbs into the tub, and I follow. I snug up against him, my back to Max's front, and then I let out a sigh of contentment.

"This is really nice," Max murmurs, his chest vibrating against me. "Having you all naked and slippery is almost as fun as having you tied up for me."

"I don't know about that," I chuckle.

"Hey, thanks for putting up with me this week. I know I've been a total drag."

Max strokes a finger slowly up and down my arm and kisses the side of my neck.

"You were dealt a major blow, love. I understand it taking you some time to cope." I reach back and loop my arms around his neck and close my eyes, so I can just enjoy the closeness.

I know I told Beck I'd have to convince Max to move to New York if things went badly at the custody hearing. I still think I should, but every time I try to find the words, the time feels wrong, or the words aren't right, or I just plain chicken out.

"I stopped by and saw my mom after work today," Max tells me.

"Did you tell her about Gigi?"

"Yeah, she cried. I felt so bad breaking her heart like that."

"I'm sorry. You don't have anything to feel bad about. If anyone should feel bad, it's Jess," I point out.

"The situation sucks, but I understand her side, too. I know if it were only up to her, she wouldn't be taking Gigi away."

"I know, but I need someone to blame for a little bit longer," I admit, and Max chuckles.

"I also told my mom about you and me."

"What?" I gasp, craning my neck to look at him. "Are you serious?"

"Yeah. She was a little weird at first, but after I explained things, I think she realized that this is what makes me happy."

"That's so great, love. I'm proud of you." I kiss him on the cheek.

"She wants us to go over there for dinner next

weekend."

"Okay," I agree. "Oh, that reminds me, Beck wants us to go out with the guys again Friday. Are you up for it?"

"Absolutely. I want to be out to them. There's no reason for us to hide what we have," Max says resolutely.

"We don't have to rush anything. We can take things at whatever pace you're comfortable with," I assure him.

"I know; I'm ready to tell our friends. Beck already knows, which means Gage must know. And who knows who he's told."

"Gage isn't a gossip."

"I know. I don't want to hide how I feel about you."

"Okay," I agree again with a smile. "Then we'll go on Friday, and I'll get to hold your hand in public and everything."

"Whatever you want, petal."

Max

"Mmm, don't you look sexy," Clay notes, peeking into my bedroom as I finish getting dressed to go out with the guys tonight.

I don't know why, but I'm nervous. I've hung out with these guys a hundred times. But now, I guess I feel like I need their approval. Clay had no problem blending into the tight knit group from the start; now, it's like I need their blessing to date him.

"Thank you. You look great, too."

Clay walks over and stands in front of the mirror with me. He tilts his head to rest on my shoulder, and he gazes at our reflection.

"We look good together. We complement each other, you know?" Clay says.

"Yeah, we do," I agree.

"Are you sure you're ready to be open in front of our friends...and out in public at the bar?" Clay checks, looking up at me with concern.

"I am. You don't deserve to be a secret, and I'm not going to treat you like one." I tilt his face and press my lips against his. "Are you ready to go?"

"Yup."

This time, Clay doesn't falter when I hand him a motorcycle jacket and helmet. He does still stumble as he mounts the bike behind me, but that's just cute as hell.

It doesn't take long for us to hit O'Malley's.

I help Clay off the bike, but really, it's more of an excuse to put my hands on him and pull him close. Clay smiles up at me, and it does funny things to my heart. I think again about what Gigi asked a few weeks ago. I know I love Clay. But, can I see building a life with him?

I trace my thumb along his bottom lip before leaning in and capturing it between my teeth. Clay sighs into my mouth and melts against me. And every cell in my body screams a resounding *yes* to both questions.

Clay's tongue meets mine, and I pull his body against me.

"I see you've found the answers to those questions you were asking at Heathens," Royal comments, slapping me on the back and forcing me to release Clay and catch my balance.

"I guess I did," I chuckle as I put my arm over Clay's shoulders, and we start walking toward the entrance to the bar.

Inside, it's easy to spot the group. Beck jumps up from his spot beside Gage and rushes over to greet us. I can never believe how fast he can move in those three-inch heels. But Gage certainly seems to appreciate the fashion choices Beck makes, as he eyes him appreciatively from behind.

"Honey, what's your secret to keep your man looking at you like that?" Clay asks Beck with a laugh.

"He knows what I'm wearing under these jeans," Beck says, turning his back to us and shimmying his ass in our direction.

"It doesn't look like you could be wearing much of anything."

"Exactly." Beck winks.

"So, are you two together now?" Adam asks, eyeing our joined hands, when Clay and I reach the table.

Clay casts a look at me like he thinks I'm suddenly going to freak out about being questioned about our relationship.

"Yeah," I confirm. "We've been dating for a few months now."

"If you need help locating the prostate, just give me a shout. I can explain everything you need to know," Royal offers with a smirk.

"He's very good at it," Zade affirms with a solemn nod.

Nash shakes his head at his boyfriends and offers me an apologetic smile.

"Please excuse them; they were obviously both raised by wolves."

Royal and Zade share a look before they both throw their heads back and start to howl in tandem.

Nash looks between his men and starts to laugh, clearly past the point of being able to rein them in.

After that, everyone seems to return to the conversations they were having before Clay and I arrived. I breathe a sigh of relief. That was so much easier than I expected it to be. Not that I thought these guys would grill me. But part of me expected it to be slightly more climactic.

"Why don't I go grab us each a drink?" I offer and Clay nods.

Now, if coming out to my brothers goes this smoothly, then I'll be in the clear. I'm not holding my breath.

CHAPTER 21

Clay

"My mom said I have to pack up all my stuff, so we can move it to our new house," Gigi says conversationally as I paint her toenails. Apparently, she likes nail polish again. It's nearly impossible to keep up with the whims of a seven-year-old.

"Are you excited about your new house?" I ask, ignoring the twinge of pain in my heart.

Gigi shrugs. "I've never moved before. What if I don't like it? Do you think we can come back if my new room doesn't feel the same?"

"I don't think so, sweetie. But don't worry, I bet your mom will let you decorate it however you want."

"Have you moved before?" Gigi asks.

"Sure, I've lived in a lot of different houses."

"But, have you moved far like I am?"

"No. I've only lived in this city. I even went to college right here."

"Why?" She cocks her head to one side when she asks.

Her question catches me off guard, and I'm not sure how to answer. The truth is, I've never moved because I was afraid. I was *terrified* of the idea. The thought of the stress of trying to find an apartment in a different city, learn new streets, find a new grocery store...the whole thing is just too much. I can almost feel hives forming at the mere thought.

"I just haven't."

"I wish you were moving with me," Gigi says sadly.

"Me too, sweetie."

"Do you think my daddy will come with me if I ask him to?"

Another sharp stab right to my heart. "Maybe," I reply in a whisper, unable to get my voice to co-operate in the face of a sudden tightening in my throat.

"Would you miss my daddy if he moved and you stayed here?"

"Very much. And I think that's enough questions for today, G. Why don't we put on a movie?"

"*Frozen*?"

"Sure. Sit still and don't smear your pretty toes. I'll put it on."

Max

It was more difficult than usual dropping Gigi back off at Jess' today after a few days together. Our time is ticking down. Only a week now before they're gone, and I won't see Gigi again until Christmas.

"Are you okay, love?" Clay asks as he pulls his car into my parents' driveway.

I shrug and give him a weak smile.

"Not so much. But at least feeling sad over Gigi has kept me from worrying about how my brothers are going to react today."

"There's always a silver lining," Clay agrees with a laugh. "Are you sure you want to do this? What if...what if things don't work out between us? Maybe you should wait to tell them for a little longer."

I grab Clay's hand and kiss his fingers. "None of that bullshit talk. I'm not letting you get away, and I have no problem telling my brothers where to shove it if they have an issue with it."

"Okay, let's do this then."

We get out of the car and head into my parents' house. I'm not surprised to find my mom in the kitchen and my dad watching baseball game.

"Clay, it's so good to see you again," My mom greets Clay with a hug.

"It's good to see you too Mrs. Moretti." Clay hugs her back.

"None of that formal stuff. You mean a lot to my Max. You'll call me Mama M from now on," she insists.

"You got it, Mama M."

My chest warms as I watch the two of them together.

"Are Gio and Tony out in the garage?" I ask my mom.

"Of course. Where else would they be?"

"Okay, I'm going to go chat with them. Are you

okay in here with my mom?" I ask Clay.

"Of course. Unless you want me there with you?"

"I'll be all right." I kiss Clay on the cheek and then head out to face my brothers.

When I was young, I was always jealous of how close those two were. I never quite fit in, and, maybe now, I know why. "Hey guys," I greet them with a nod.

"You don't usually slum it out here with us. What's up?" Gio asks.

"There's something I wanted to talk to you guys about."

"Go for it, bro," Tony prompts.

I take a deep breath and wipe my sweaty palms on my jeans. Ma already said she has my back, and it's not like Gio and Tony are going to *do* anything to me. But I can't help feeling like I'm about to put an even bigger divide between my brothers and myself.

"Here's the thing guys…" I clear my throat and glance down at my shoes. "I've been seeing someone, and it's pretty serious."

"Oh yeah?" Gio perks up. "This the chick who's had you smiling for a few months?"

"You look nervous; you knock her up?" Tony pipes in with a snicker.

"Nobody's knocked up," I grumble. "And nobody's *gonna* get knocked up because I'm dating Clay."

Stunned silence is about what I expected, and my brothers don't disappoint. I chance a look at them and find them both gaping at me like I've grown an extra head.

"You're shitting us," Tony guesses weakly.

"Nope." I shake my head and square my shoulders to prepare for the inevitable onslaught that'll come as soon as they realize what I'm telling them.

"You're a queer?" Gio asks with quiet confusion.

The word isn't said with venom, so I keep my own tone even when I answer. "I told you not to use that word, Gio."

"Okay, but are you?"

"I don't really know," I admit. "I still like women, and I like Clay." I shrug.

"But he's a guy," Tony points out, making me chuckle.

"Yeah, I noticed that."

"I don't get it," Gio admits.

"Okay, it's like, imagine if someone gave you a fully restored 1963 Corvette Stingray Split Window Coupe but instead of being red like you always pictured, it was black. Would you send it back?" Gio and Tony both shake their head at the sacrilegious idea. "That's exactly what this is like. Clay is everything I ever wanted. He's everything I was missing in every woman I ever dated. Did I expect my soulmate to have a dick? No. But, hell, my own was always fun enough to play with; now, I've got a spare."

Gio cracks a smile, and Tony still looks bewildered, but I can tell my words registered on some level.

"I guess that makes sense," Gio admits.

I breathe a sigh of relief and pull my brother into a hug. Gio squeezes back and claps me on the back.

When I release him, I turn to Tony, weary of what I might find there.

"As long as you don't tell me what you two do in bed, I can live with it," Tony concedes.

I roll my eyes at him. "Dude, like I want to tell you about my sex life anyway. You're the one who thinks everyone needs a play by play."

Tony chuckles. "That's fair," he agrees, and then he opens his arms for a hug too.

Once the Kumbaya moment is over, the three of us head inside for dinner.

Clay is in the middle of helping my mom put the finishing touches on some sort of chocolate dessert, and he raises an eyebrow in question as soon as he sees me.

With my brothers right behind me, I stride over to Clay and pull him into a kiss, letting my tongue sweep briefly into his mouth.

"Mmm, you taste like chocolate," I note, bumping my nose against Clay's in an affectionate gesture.

"You taste like giant, sexy man," Clay teases.

"Get a room," Gio complains, and Tony chuckles.

My dad comes over and claps me on the shoulder without comment. I guess my mom decided to take one thing off my plate for me after all.

We all sit down around the table and Ma fills our plates.

"Hey, bro, you know my friend, Ace, is still bugging me about you," Tony says as we all start digging into dinner.

"I told you I'm not interested."

"Interested in what?" Clay asks.

"Nothing," I shoot Tony a warning look that he chooses to ignore.

"My buddy owns a custom bike shop and he wants to talk to Max about a job."

"Oh my god, that's amazing. Why aren't you interested?" Clay asks.

"Because, it's three-thousand miles away."

Clay's face falls and something dark passes behind his eyes. "Where is it?"

"Philadelphia," Tony tells him.

"See, that would never work. Now, can we change the subject?" I insist.

Clay

My chest tightens, and the back of my throat starts to ache as I attempt to keep my breathing even. All the sounds around me swirl and seem to intensify. It's like if you put on ten different songs all at once and then crank the volume up as loud as it will go.

"Excuse me," I say quietly, getting up from the table where the subject has moved on to something about cars or sports...I don't honestly know. All I know is that the bile is rising in my throat, and I can't think straight. I ignore the questioning look Max gives me, and I rush to the bathroom.

I lock the door and hunch over the sink as I

try to get my bearings.

I knew if Jess won custody I'd have to give Max up. I knew it was the only right thing to do. But, selfishly I'd hoped there would be some excuse to keep him here with me. Knowing now that not only is his daughter going to be on the East Coast, but his dream job too? He has to go. And based on his reaction at the table, I'm going to have to give him a push out the door.

A knock comes at the bathroom door.

"Are you okay, petal?"

"Fine. I'll be right out," I lie before splashing some cold water on my face and crouching down for a few seconds. Then, I stand back up and take a deep breath. It's game face time.

I step out of the bathroom and am met by a concerned look all over Max's face.

"I just felt sick for a second; I'm fine," I assure him.

"You want to call it an early night? If you're not feeling well, I should take you home."

"We can finish dinner and then go home," I assure him.

###

When we pull up at home an hour later, my mouth is dry, and my heart is flailing in my chest as I take Max's hand. Everything in me is resisting what I'm about to suggest. But I know it's the right thing.

"Can we sit down and talk for a minute?" I

ask as we walk inside.

"Sure. Is something wrong?" Max sits down on the couch and tugs me down beside him.

"I've been thinking about everything with Gigi, and I think—" My voice fails me as my eyes start to burn. "I think you need to go."

"Go where?"

"To New York. Or, uh, to Philadelphia. I looked it up and if you moved to New Jersey you could be like an hour from New York City and a half hour from Philadelphia. So, you could take that great job, and get Gigi every weekend. It would be perfect."

"When did you look it up?" he asks with a hint of annoyance.

"After dinner, right before dessert. When I went to the bathroom a second time, I looked it up on my phone," I explain. "But I'm serious, you have to go."

"But what about you?" Max asks in a shaky voice.

"I've got my studio here, love. We can try long distance and see how things go?" I suggest, not fully believing that will work long term, but also not willing to give up on Max just yet.

"Petal," Max lifts his hands up to cup my face. "I love you. I'm in love with you. I can't leave you."

A sob bursts from my chest. Why the hell does life have to be so cruel? It figures I'd finally find the perfect man, just to have to give him up.

"I love you, too. But you need to go be with your daughter. If things are meant to be between us, we'll find a way."

Max pulls me into his arms, and I melt against his strong chest. "I'm not giving you up, so I hope you're prepared to FaceTime daily."

"You bet your ass," I agree with a tearful laugh.

CHAPTER 22

Clay

"Clay, how could you let him go like this?" Beck asks sadly, placing a hand over mine.

"I have to. He needs to be with Gigi."

"I agree; he needs to move to the East Coast. But I don't understand why your dumb ass is staying here."

"Please, that's crazy talk," I scoff. "First of all, we've been dating a few months. I can't move across the country with him. I dated Jake for years, and I didn't move with him either. And while we're on that subject, what's the deal with every guy I fall in love with moving east?"

"You're an idiot. You weren't meant to move with Jake. Max is your person, should move now."

"It's not going to happen. Drop it, okay?" I snap as my chest tightens. I can't handle talking about this anymore. "I'm going to go look at apartments with him this weekend, and then I'm going to come home and that will be that."

"Okay, but where are you going to live?"

"Max is signing over the lease on our place into my name. I can get a roommate if I need to."

"If this is what you want, then I'll shut up. If you need anything, you know I'm here for you."

I nod and wipe away the moisture forming in the corner of my eye. "Do you mind if I take off a little early? I haven't stopped over at my mom's place recently, and I could use a visit."

"Yeah, get out of here. I can handle everything here," Beck assures me, waving me toward the door.

At my mom's house, I walk in without knocking like I've always done.

"Mom, are you home?" I call out as I place my shoes on the mat by the door.

"I'm in the living room."

I follow her voice and find her doing yoga in the middle of the living room. At least I come by it honestly.

"You're doing that pose wrong; you're going to hurt yourself," I admonish before helping her reposition her feet so she has the correct stance.

"Thanks sweetie. What brings you by? Usually, you're too busy for your poor old mom."

"I've been seeing someone."

"That's great news." She straightens up and beams at me. "It's been years since you've been serious with anyone. Not since Jake, right?"

"Yup, I'm a pretty big loser," I confirm.

"You're not a loser. You're special, and most men can't see it," she corrects. "Does this new guy

217

know how special you are?"

"He does. It's my roommate, Max."

"That's fantastic. I'm betting you got a big *I told you so* from Beck?"

"Of course. The thing is, he's moving this weekend. His ex is getting married and taking his daughter to the East Coast, and I told Max he has to go with."

My mom's face falls. "You don't want to move?"

"No, I'm happy here." I shake my head. "I'm comfortable here," I correct after a second.

My mom sighs and puts her arms around me. "You always were a twitchy, nervous kid. I'm sorry if your anxiety is my fault."

I laugh through the tears that are forming. "No, Mom. I think my brain is just fucked up. It's not your fault."

"You are not *fucked up*."

"Whatever you say, Mom."

Max

I look around my barren room and my gut twists. Leaving Clay feels all kinds of wrong. But letting Gigi go doesn't feel right either. No matter what choice I make, I lose one of the most important people in my life.

I've made a decision, though, and now I need to make the best of it.

"It looks a lot bigger in here without all your stuff," Clay says, his voice rough and quiet as he stands in the doorway to my room.

"I know; it's weird."

"The Uber should be here in a minute. Are you ready to go?"

"I guess so. Everything is loaded in the Pod, which will be delivered in a few days. We just need to get out there and find a place I can rent. I got ahold of Ace; he says he's looking forward to meeting with me and talking about the job he's got open at his shop."

"That's great. This is the right decision," Clay says almost like he's trying to convince himself.

CHAPTER 23

Clay

I close my eyes and try to focus on my breathing.

"You okay, petal?" Max asks with concern, reaching over the armrest and squeezing my hand.

"I've never been on a plane before," I admit. "I've...uh...never left Seattle before, actually."

"Seriously?"

I nod, breathing in through my nose and out through my mouth.

"Hey, petal, open your eyes and look at me for a second," Max says in the authoritative voice he normally only uses during sexy times.

I pry my lids open and focus on looking right into Clay's captivating, dark eyes.

"I'm scared," I admit needlessly.

"I know, petal." Max lifts a hand to my face and cups my jaw, rubbing his thumb along my cheek. I relax into his touch, the contact making me feel better instantly. "You're not going to worry about this. Just like when I bind you, you're going to give all your worries over to me and let me be responsible for anything stressful. Can you be good and do that for me?"

My breath catches in my chest, and I can feel tears

of relief burning in my eyes. "God yes," I breathe out slowly, looking at my strong, confident lover and knowing he's more than capable of shouldering the things I'm giving up worrying over. "How do you always know what I need?"

"Because you're mine, and it's my job to know."

It's on the tip of my tongue to take back this whole stupid idea of Max moving without me. I want to beg him not to leave me behind.

Just then the flight attendant starts giving instructions, and I'm saved from saying something embarrassing to Max.

Max

Every place we look at feels wrong. They're all too cold, too empty, too...blah.

"We'll make it homey," Clay argues as we stand in the middle of the seventh apartment we've looked at this weekend. "I'll help you decorate before I leave."

My chest aches at his words. That's the problem. These places are all fine, but the fact that I'll be living in whichever one I choose without Clay? That's almost unbearable.

"Fine. This is fine, I guess. It doesn't matter," I sigh. The realtor who's been showing us around all day visibly relaxes.

"I'll get you the rental agreement for this one. If you're approved, you can move in as soon as next week."

"Perfect," I mumble.

"Love," Clay puts his arms around my waist and looks up at me. "This place is great. There's an extra bedroom for Gigi and you have your own garage to keep your bike in and still have room to work on your side projects out there. You'll be happy here."

"Yeah," I agree without feeling. "Let's get this paperwork filled out and go back to the hotel to spend time just the two of us."

Clay

"I got you a little present," Max tells me when we get back to the hotel.

"Why would you get me a present?" I ask in pleasant surprise.

"It's really for both of us," Max admits with a little pink creeping into his cheeks as he hands me a small gift bag.

I pull the tissue paper out and reach inside. My fingers brush against the unmistakable feel of silky soft ropes, and my cock instantly starts to fill. I pull out the ropes, my heart beating hard against my ribs. Unlike my black ropes, these are a number of vibrant colored bindings.

"I've been doing a lot of research, and you wouldn't believe how beautiful the Shibari pictures look when you use colored ropes. And everything I read said that when we can't be together, looking at pictures of our past sessions will put us both in that familiar headspace. These are made of bamboo silk; they're some of the softest ropes

I could find. And, if it's okay, I'd love to try some more complicated binding designs and then take pictures of you for us both to enjoy when we're apart."

The idea of having pictures of me bound for Max is enough to make me dizzy with pleasure. "Can we start now?"

Max chuckles and then scoops me up into his arms. "Anything you want, petal."

He deposits me gently onto the bed and then starts pulling out all the different colored ropes and laying them beside me. Max looks them over carefully before choosing a few.

"You might want to limber up before we get started, petal. I'm going to test your limits tonight."

A soft moan escapes my lips. "God, yes."

"Strip for me."

I scramble onto my knees on the bed and hurry to pull my shirt over my head and toss it aside. My pants and underwear join my shirt on the floor seconds later.

My cock is already hard, bobbing free in front of me as I kneel in the center of the bed.

"So beautiful and eager for me," Max says as his eyes roam greedily over my body. "The things I'm going to do to you tonight, petal…"

"Stop teasing and tie me up already," I beg, crawling toward him.

"Patience." His voice is deep and commanding, sending a shiver through me and leaving no room for argument. "I'm going to play with you for hours before either of us get to come."

My cock jerks at his words, my breath catching.

"Stay just like this for me, petal," Max instructs as he trails a finger from my collarbone to my hip, leaving goosebumps in his wake. "Just spread your legs a little wider for me."

I shuffle my knees farther apart. Max takes a length of powder blue rope and loops it around my right thigh. He winds it around and around, his fingers occasionally brushing against my balls, making me squirm and whimper. After a few times around, he grabs a hot pink rope and ties the two together, creating a knot in the center of the rope already wound around my thigh. He runs the pink rope up to my hip and wraps that around my middle in an intricate pattern.

I can't tear my eyes away from his rough, calloused fingers as he works. It seems strange that a man with such large hands could use them so nimbly. Yet Max works the ropes like he's been doing this for years.

My cock strains to be touched as Max ties in a third rope—this one royal blue.

"Grab your wrists for me," he instructs. I obey, and Max leans in and flicks his tongue along the column of my throat.

Within a few minutes, my wrists are bound together and connected to the binding from my hips to my thigh. The next rope that's added is a lighter pink. Max works it into the knot around my wrists and then drags the soft rope over my chest and over my shoulder.

"Almost finished with the first one, petal," Max assures me before reaching between my legs and tenderly cupping my balls. He rolls them in his palm and kisses along my jaw with sloppy, open mouthed kisses.

My chest heaves as I try to draw in breaths, my cock dripping pre-cum onto Max's forearm as he plays with my balls.

As abruptly as it started, Max's touch is gone and he's moving around behind me on the bed. I can feel as he works the rope along my back and ties it into the original knot around my thigh.

"So beautiful, petal. Do you have any idea how crazy I am about you?" Max asks as he rubs the rough stubble of his cheek against my shoulder blades.

"I love you," I choke out.

"Oh petal, I'm so in love with you."

A sob breaks free from my throat, and I'm sure the only thing keeping me from shattering into a million pieces are the ropes binding me and Max's strong presence at my back.

"Don't cry," Max soothes. "We're only making happy memories tonight."

I nod, pinching my eyes closed and willing the tears to recede. Max stays put at my back, running soothing hands over my skin and brushing kisses against my neck until my body starts to relax again.

When he pulls out his camera, my body heats as I imagine Max alone in his bed, getting off to pictures of me bound for him.

He snaps countless pictures over the next few hours. Each time untying me afterward and starting all over again. I lost count of how many ways he bound me and how much time passed before he finally thrust inside me.

I sob with relief, my cock beyond painfully hard and my balls sore from being held off so long.

As soon as he's inside me, I can feel him stiff and throbbing.

"I can't—" Max groans, pulling back and slamming his hips against my ass hard enough to make me gasp.

"Don't hold back; I can't wait," I agree.

Max grunts and grinds himself deeper inside me. He pulls out and slams home again, this time his broad head slides against my prostate, and my body explodes. My balls tighten, and my cock heaves as the most intense orgasm I've ever felt barrels through me.

Max lets out a strangled cry and pumps his hot seed deep inside me.

I'm still trembling from aftershocks when Max unties me. I can't even bring myself to move as he wipes me off, positions me in the center of the bed, and then climbs in beside me.

I'm asleep before I can even count a hundred heartbeats.

CHAPTER 24

Max

I shift against the rough sheets of the hotel bed and watch as the morning sun slowly creeps over Clay's smooth skin.

My heart is breaking painfully inside my chest at the thought of seeing Clay off to the airport today.

He said we'd find a way to make this work, and I *want* to believe him. I can't let him go. I've never felt this way about anyone before. I've never come close to feeling this way. I know his studio and his life are back in Seattle. It would be selfish of me to beg him to stay. Even knowing that, I want to get down on my hands and knees and plead with him.

"I thought you said we were only doing happy thoughts," Clay says in a sleepy voice.

"I don't want to think about letting you go."

"This is for the best. You get to be here with Gigi; that's the important thing."

"You'll come to visit, right? And I'll come out to see you?" I ask, grasping desperately for reassurance that this isn't the last time I'll have Clay in my bed.

He gives me a sad smile and runs his fingers through my messy hair. "Of course, love." His words don't reassure me like I want them to. "Why don't we get up and share a shower and breakfast before I have to catch my flight?"

Clay

I bite down on my bottom lip, trying hard to keep the tears at bay. The last thing Max needs is for me to turn into a blubbering mess when he's trying to be strong and tell me goodbye.

Goodbye—What an asshole of a word it is.

"Petal, I hate this." Max grabs my hand and looks into my eyes. His deep brown eyes are glassy with unshed tears and red rimmed. "Stay. Please stay."

"I...can't."

Max nods and looks down at his feet. When he looks back up, there's a smile plastered on his lips. "Call me when you get home, okay? And we'll FaceTime every day. We'll organize visits, so we can see each other every few months. This is going to be fine." Max's voice has a high desperate quality that breaks my heart in two.

"Yeah, this will be easy," I lie.

Max squeezes my hand and then leans in and kisses me slowly and so sweet it makes my knees weak. I clutch Max to me and memorize the taste of his lips. This may be the last time. His lips are so soft as they move against mine. I need to lock this feeling up in my mind and never let it go.

"I love you," I whisper against his lips.

"I love you so much, petal. More than I ever

thought possible."

I barely keep it together as I board the plane. And as soon as I'm in my seat, the tears start to fall. I wrap my arms around myself and close my eyes, trying to keep the image of Max in my mind.

"Leaving someone special behind?" a woman asks from beside me.

I don't bother to open my eyes; I just nod and turn my head toward the window.

Max

Watching Clay board the plane, it feels like my heart is being ripped out of my chest.

I pull out my phone and dial Jess. "Hey, mind if I come up and see Gigi tonight?"

"Sure. Did you just see Clay off?" she asks with sympathy in her tone.

"Yeah." I swallow hard, my grip on my phone tightening. I want to run after him, beg him to stay. "I'll be there in an hour."

"Okay. You can stay the night in our guest room if you want. Your place isn't ready yet, is it?"

"I can't move in for two more days. I appreciate the offer. I'll see you soon."

###

Jess and Mark are generous enough to let me spend some time at their place while I wait to move into my new apartment. A few days after Clay went home, I realized I was going to have to get a car of my own now. I picked up a responsible, reliable little sedan to be able to drive Gigi around in. It felt all kinds of wrong to get a car. It felt like admitting I really do have to do this without Clay after all. I never realized how much he did to help me out with Gigi until he was on the other side of the country.

I wake up on my last day at their place, ready to take Gigi on a trip to the aquarium that I promised her at the beginning of the week.

"Are you excited to go to the Adventure Aquarium today?" I ask her.

"Yeah, I want to see a dolphin."

After a several minutes search for Gigi's new favorite stuffed animal that she just couldn't leave for the day, we're on the road on the way to the aquarium.

"What's your favorite fish, Daddy?" Gigi asks from the backseat.

"I like sharks."

"Sharks are scary," Gigi argues.

"Animals are only scary if you bother them. If you respect their environment and stay away from them, then they're safe."

"What's Clay's favorite fish?" Gigi asks, and the familiar lonely ache invades my chest. It's only been a few days away from Clay, and I miss him so much it's like a physical pain.

"I'm not sure sweetie, maybe after the aquarium we can call him tonight and ask."

"Yeah!" Gigi agrees with excitement. "Can he read me a bedtime story over the phone."

"I'm sure he will."

"I wish Clay was here," Gigi says.

"Me too, princess," I agree with a sigh.

###

The only place I've worked in my life is the garage owned by my own father. And I only met Ace once for about a half hour before he offered me the job.

As I pull into the parking lot of the custom bike shop where I now work, I feel my phone vibrate in my pocket.

> **Petal:** Good luck on your first day at your new job. You're going to be so happy. I love you.
>
> **Max:** Thanks petal. I miss you like crazy.
>
> **Petal:** Hey, none of that. Go have a good day.
>
> **Max:** K

I shove my phone back into my pocket and head into the garage.

It's not like I'm used to. It's so much more modern and shiny inside than Moretti Motors was even in its heyday I'm sure.

"Hey, Max," Ace calls out a greeting from where he's working on the frame of a Harley by the looks of it.

Ace is pretty much everything I expected from a guy who owns his own custom bike shop. He's a big guy, rough around the edges and covered in ink. His hair is a green mohawk that's currently flopped over to one side rather than styled to stand up straight. And he's got a septum piercing.

When I showed Clay a picture, he declared Ace to be a *major hottie*. I don't know if Ace just isn't my type or if Clay is the only man who does it for me. I'm with Clay so the rest of it doesn't matter.

"Hey, man." I walk over and look at what he's working on.

"I'm stoked to have you here. I've got the perfect bike for you to start on. Come on, let me show you."

He talks me through a custom build that was just placed two days ago that he thought I'd be perfect for. And as he describes what the owner wants, I can feel my excitement bubbling beneath the surface.

This is a dream come true. This is everything I ever wanted when I was a kid in the garage figuring out how to put a motorcycle back together.

If only Clay were here.

I get to work, and over the next few hours, Ace and I chat across the shop when we can manage it over the sound of our tools.

"How are you getting moved in this weekend all by yourself?" Ace asks after I tell him that I got approved for the apartment and am getting settled on my next day off.

"I'll figure it out," I shrug.

"Fuck that; I'll help. I'm not doing anything, might as well get a good workout hauling furniture and shit."

"Thanks man, I appreciate that."

"Don't mention it."

CLAY

My chest feels tight, my shoulders are tense, and the buzzing in my brain is louder than ever.

My phone rings with my FaceTime notification, and I jump to grab it, expecting it to be Max. My shoulders sag a little when I realize it's Jake.

I accept the call and plaster on a smile. "Hey, how's it going?"

"You look like shit."

"Gee thanks," I respond sarcastically.

"Seriously, babe. Is something wrong?"

I flop down on the couch in my painfully empty place and sigh loudly.

"Things got serious with my roommate, Max. I fell in love with him," I admit.

"That's great."

"No, he had to move to New Jersey."

"No shit? That's where I live now. I should meet up with him, we can commiserate over having loved and lost the one and only Clay Rollins."

"Why is life so shitty?" I sigh.

"I don't know. But, one thing I've learned since I let you go...if you love someone, you have to fight for them."

My heart squeezes in my chest, and I nod sadly.

"This isn't a great time, I was just on my way out. Can I call you back another day?"

"Sure, babe. Take care of yourself." Jake blows me a kiss before signing off.

I toss my phone down and curl onto my side, pulling my legs up to my chest, and start to cry.

CHAPTER 25

Max

I run my hand along the smooth body of the custom Ducati that I put together with my own hands. And I got paid to do it! It's like a dream come true...if only Clay were here with me.

"What's wrong, man?" Ace asks. "The bike looks kick ass, why are you frowning?"

"Ah, it's nothing," I wave him off, refusing to acknowledge the heavy stone in the pit of my stomach every time I think of Clay.

"Girl trouble?" Ace guesses with a smirk.

"Guy, actually. And not *trouble* exactly. I just miss him since moving is all."

"Oh, I didn't know you were gay."

"I don't like labels. But I *am* dating a man." I shrug, surprising myself a bit with my casual honesty. In the past, the thought of talking so openly about my sexuality and about Clay would've sent me into a cold sweat. But being away from him, missing him so much, has changed a lot it seems.

"That's cool, dude. I watched gay porn once. The dude really knew how to suck a dick."

I bark out a laugh and shake my head at Ace. At least, he's being supportive?

"Well, not a lot of dick sucking going on right now for me. Clay is still back in Seattle, and he doesn't have any immediate plans to move out here."

"Oh man, that's rough," Ace shakes his head and pats me on the shoulder. "You never know, maybe he's missing you as much as you're missing him."

"I hope so," I agree with a chuckle.

"Seriously though, this bike is sick; the client is going to love it."

"Thanks."

"Any time. And I hope when your man comes to visit, you can manage to make it out of bed long enough to introduce me."

"I promise to try."

Ace holds his hand out for a fist bump, which I gladly give. Then, we both return to our respective projects.

On the way home, I pass a small pub and decide to pull in to grab a drink.

"Can I get whatever's on tap?" I request, sliding onto a barstool.

The bartender nods and turns to get me a drink while I glance around the small bar. It's nothing like O'Malley's. There's no Beau, no guys from Heathens, and most importantly, there's no Clay.

My chest aches at the distance between us. It's only been three weeks, and I'm not sure how much longer I can stand to be away from him. Before this, I hadn't gone a single day without seeing Clay since we met. Sure, we weren't together for the first five years, but we were in almost every part of each other's daily lives. He was just *there*, his presence permeating every part of me and slowly forcing me to fall in love with him long before I ever realized it.

"You look familiar; do I know you?" A lanky, blond man asks, sliding onto the stool beside me and eyeing me with interest.

"I doubt it; I just moved here a few weeks ago from Seattle."

The man's eyes light up. "Wait, you're not Max, are you?"

"Yes?" I answer warily.

"Clay's boyfriend, Max?"

"Yeah. I'm sorry, who the hell are you?"

The man chuckles and then offers me his hand. "I'm Jake, Clay's ex. I've seen you all over Clay's Facebook."

"Oh," I search my mind for any mention of a Jake and then... "*Oh*."

"I'm assuming he mentioned me at some point?"

"Once or twice," I mutter.

"Well, welcome to the club, I guess."

"What club?" I ask.

"The club for guys who regret letting Clay get away."

"I didn't let him get away. We're still together," I snap, refusing to acknowledge the sore spot his words just hit.

"Sure, for now. But how's that going to work long term? He's not leaving Seattle. I tried to convince him to a decade ago, and he refused. Now he's got even more reason to stay there, with his business and everything. You may not be calling time of death yet, but your relationship is on life support, without a doubt."

"Listen asshole, you don't know shit about me. And you may have dated Clay a lifetime ago, but you don't know him as well as you think you do either. We're going to find a way to make this work," I insist.

"I wish you the best of luck," Jake tips his drink at me and then gives me a pitying smile before strolling away.

I stay at the bar for just one drink before heading home to my silent apartment. I never noticed how much Clay's presence added to our home in Seattle. Even before I realized what he meant to me, his presence was comforting.

"Where are we going with this?" Ace asks, walking backward into my apartment, carrying one side of my dresser.

"This is going on the far wall of the bedroom."

After finagling it around the corner of the hallway, we manage to get it into my room and placed along the far wall, beneath the window.

Ace pulls in a deep breath and wipes his arm along his sweaty brow.

"Damn, I need to quit smoking."

Ace glances around my room, casually looking at the boxes that are mostly half unpacked, items strewn about.

"What do we have here?" he asks with interest, walking over to the box nearest my closet and picking up one of the pink ropes from inside.

Seeing his hands all over my ropes, *Clay's* ropes, causes my gut to clench. I stride across the room and yank the rope from his hands.

"Don't touch that," I snap, before laying it back in the box gently.

"Whoa, sorry." Ace holds his hands up and gives me an apologetic look. "I shouldn't be snooping."

"Sorry, I didn't mean to get so pissy; it's just...imagine if someone was pawing through your girlfriend's underwear."

"I don't have a girlfriend, but point taken. It's something personal, and I shouldn't be touching it."

I nod and pat Ace on the shoulder to let him know there are no hard feelings.

"All right, the couch is up next, right?"

"Yup, let's get this done so we can have some beer and pizza."

Clay

I'm folded into *Marichyasana I* pose, trying to ignore Beck's mumbled jabs about me being a human pretzel and the incessant buzzing in my brain that's worse than ever since Max left. I'm up to yoga three times daily, and every inch of the house is sparkling clean. Nothing is working to settle me. I haven't slept for more than a few hours a night since I got back to Seattle.

"You okay?" Beck asks.

"Fucking great," I growl sarcastically as I shift into *Paschimottanasana.*

"Have you talked to Max since he moved?"

"Yeah, he's settling in. He likes his new job. It was the right decision."

"I never doubted that. I'm just still trying to figure out what you're still doing here."

"It's not that simple," I snap. "Can we please just drop this?"

Clay mimes zipping his lips.

After our morning yoga, I'm able to keep myself busy most of the day with classes and the endless administrative crap that always piles up. But as the day turns into night, and the last class files out, I find myself behind my desk in my office, for once desperately trying to think of something to do that will keep me here instead of having to go home to the painfully quiet house.

"I thought you left ages ago," Beck says, popping his head in.

"Nope. Leaving in a few minutes though," I lie.

"Okay, I'm heading out. Call me if you need anything."

"Have a good night."

"You too," Beck calls back on his way out.

Alone in the studio, it's just as oppressively quiet as it would be at home.

I stand up and pace around my office, straightening things as I move. Then it occurs to me that it's been ages since I've given the studio a deep clean. What better night for it than this?

I grab my cleaning supplies from the bathroom off my office, and I head into studio one.

I wipe down the mirrored wall, careful not to leave any streaks. Then, on hands and knees, I start at one end of the studio and get to work wiping the floor down until it's pristine.

After I finish studio one, I start toward studio two when I hear my phone ringing in my office.

I set down my cleaning supplies and sprint to grab my phone before I can miss the call. I'm sure it'll be Max at this hour.

Sure enough, it's a FaceTime request from Max that I happily accept as I plop down in my chair and hold my phone in front of me.

"Hey, petal," Max greets with a sleepy smile. The background is dark, but I can tell he's lying in bed. His hair is messy across his pillow, and his lack of shirt makes me wish I was curled up next to him, feeling his warm skin against mine.

"Hey, love. I miss you."

"I miss you too," Max sighs. "Are you at the studio?" he asks.

"Yeah, I was about to go home," I lie.

"It's one in the morning. What are you doing still at the studio?"

"Just a little spring cleaning."

"It's August," he points out.

"Head start?" I try with a shrug.

"Petal," his commanding tone makes me shiver.

"I couldn't sleep. It's too quiet at home, and my bed is too big and empty. I didn't want to go back there tonight," I admit, absentmindedly straightening a few papers on my desk and shuffling the pens in my cup into groups based on color and amount of ink left.

"I should be there to take care of you," Max says quietly, and I can tell he's blaming himself.

"Don't worry about me. I'm a big boy; I'm not your concern."

"You're wrong. You *are* mine to worry about and take care of," Max growls. "You're *mine*, petal. Take off your pants."

"What?" I scoff at his command.

"I'm going to help you relax because that's my job. Now, take off your pants."

I consider arguing but decide to go with it. Although, I think it's only fair to tell Max the truth.

"I don't really jerk off. It doesn't do much for me so it's not worth the effort."

"This isn't your run of the mill jerk off session. You're going to let me take care of you, like I always do."

My cock shifts against my thigh, thickening and stiffening at the deep timbre and raw authority in his voice.

My pants pool around my ankles as I sit back down in my chair and wait for Max to tell me what he wants next.

I reach for my cock instinctively but Max stops me with a sharp reprimand.

"You're not allowed to touch your dick unless I say."

I pull my hand back, my heart thundering wildly. My cock is hard and flushed, bobbing outward.

"Lick your fingers." I do as he says, sucking my middle finger and ring finger into my mouth. "Now stick those fingers between your cute little cheeks and tell me how much your hole misses me."

"Holy shit, where did you learn all this delicious dirty talk?" I pant as I tease my fingers around my hole.

"The internet. You'd be surprised all the filthy stuff you can learn on there," Max teases and I smile.

I close my eyes and imagine his breath tickling my neck and the weight of his body pinning me down as he stretches me open.

"God, Max, I need you," I moan breathlessly as I slip my fingers inside.

"You have me."

I watch as he pans the camera down so I can see his hand working his cock and then back up to his face.

I push my fingers deeper, my free hand twitching for my cock as Max murmurs and moans encouragement. My hand twitches for my cock.

"Not yet," Max corrects. "Play with your balls."

I whine but do as he says, tugging my sac and then rolling it in my palm as I fuck myself on my other hand.

"*Max,*" I whimper. I slide farther down in my chair,

putting my feet up on my desk and giving Max an excellent view. I push my fingers deeper, gliding over my prostate and making my cock jerk. "Please."

"Grab your cock, petal."

I shudder with relief and wrap my fist around my shaft and tug it hard and fast.

"Oh fuck, oh yeah," I cry out as I fuck my fingers deeper. Pleasure coils tight in the pit of my stomach and, with one more jerk, explodes out through my entire body. Sticky white cum coats my stomach, and Max lets out a grunted groan before his lips part and his eyes roll up a little.

When his eyes focus again, he gives me a little smile. "Do you feel any better?" he asks.

"A little. I'm sleepy now. I'll probably crash in my office since it's so late."

"Take care of yourself for me petal, until you're close enough for me to do it for you."

"I'll try," I promise.

"Clay, sweetie, wake up." Beck shakes me awake and the crick in my neck makes me immediately regret sleeping at my desk.

"What time is it?" I ask, rubbing the sleep from my eyes.

"Nine. Did you sleep here all night?"

"Yeah, I didn't want to go back to the house," I admit. "It's too quiet there without

Max."

"I don't know how you're doing it. I can't imagine being on the opposite side of the country from Gage," Beck muses.

"It fucking sucks. I miss him all the time. I can't sleep, and I feel like I'm missing a limb. I don't know what to do though. Maybe it would be best if I just admit that this isn't going to work and start working on the healing process instead of hanging onto something that's not going anywhere."

"Oh, hell no," Beck snaps, crossing his arms and glaring at me. "I'm not letting you do this again."

"Do what?"

"When Jake moved to the East Coast, I always thought you should've gone with him. I get that you were afraid to leave the only place you've ever lived, and maybe Jake wasn't the right person to make that sacrifice for. But, sweetie, Max is *the one*. I can see it written all over your face and his. You two belong together, and I think you need to get your ass to New Jersey."

"What about On Pointe? What about you? I can't leave my whole life here," I argue, even as my heart starts to build a new hope for the future.

"I'll be fine. Obviously, Gage and I will come out to visit you, and you'll have to FaceTime me constantly. But you don't need to worry about me anymore like you used to. I'm happy, I'm whole, and I've got everything I need with Gage. As for On Pointe...what if I buy it from you? Then you'll know it's still being well taken care of, and you can go build a new dream with your man?"

"Seriously? You want to buy this place?"

"Yeah, I've been thinking I could do free yoga and dance classes for kids at Rainbow House and donate some profits to them as well. I also have some ideas for expanding some of the adult classes, like maybe pole dancing and stuff."

"Those are great ideas," I agree. "I can't just up and leave though," I argue again as the knot of anxiety twists in the pit of my stomach.

"Why not?" Beck demands.

"I've only ever lived here. What would I do somewhere new? I would have to get used to a whole new grocery store, and I wouldn't know where anything was."

"You are *not* letting Max get away because they don't have a fucking Albertsons on the East Coast. Jesus Clay, listen to yourself."

"It's not about the Albertsons."

"What then?" Beck demands.

"I'm terrified. I can hardly function here; how will I manage to keep it together when I'm somewhere new and different. I can't do it." I put my face in my hands and let a few tears fall as the tight, burning sensation in the back of my throat intensifies.

"Sweetie," Beck's voice is gentle as he puts a hand on my shoulder. "Do you think Max would let you fall apart? He'll be there to help you adjust. Will it be difficult at first? Of course. But you'll get used to it, and then you'll wonder what you were so afraid of to begin with."

"Maybe," I concede. "I'll think about it."

"That's better than you've been giving me, so I'll take it. Now, you need to get some sleep. Go home and rest; I'll take your classes today. And I don't want to see you back here until you look less like Nosferatu."

I snort a laugh and wipe my eyes one last time before giving Beck a hug and standing up.

"Okay, I'll see you tomorrow. Thanks for everything; I don't know what I'd do without you."

"You'd be utterly lost, obviously," Beck agrees with a smirk.

"Very true."

The fresh air outside wakes me up, and I decide to walk to the coffee shop and then head down to the park to clear my head.

Could it really be that easy just to move and trust that I'll adjust eventually? I want it to be true. I want Beck to be right.

My mind wanders back to my call with Max last night. It's just further proof that Max understands me better than I understand myself sometimes. Beck said Max would take care of me, and he has no idea how right he is. But can I lay this all on Max to deal with all my anxieties?

When I reach the park, I sit down in the grass and watch as people pass. I sip my coffee and shudder at the taste. It's not as good as Max makes. Nothing is as good without Max here.

I pull my phone out of my pocket and call my mom.

"Hello?"

"Hi, Mom. I need some advice."

"What's wrong? You sound awful."

I huff a laugh and absentmindedly wipe the specks of dirt off my shoes with my index finger.

"Do you think I should move to—"

"Absolutely," My mom cuts me off before I can finish. "Get your ass on a plane today."

"Jeez, you must be eager to get rid of me," I try to joke, but my voice is too flat.

"Never. But I do want you to be happy. You can't keep yourself in a safe little bubble here your whole life. You need to go out in the world and find your way."

"I'm scared, and Beck said I should lean on Max, but I'm worried that will create a co-dependent relationship or something."

"Leaning on your partner isn't co-dependent; it's what relationships are all about. I know I never had the chance to set many good examples for you where relationships are concerned. But love is about leaning on each other. When Max needed help with Gigi, he leaned on you, didn't he?"

"Yeah," I agree.

"See? He wasn't co-dependent; he was letting you take some of the weight he couldn't carry. He'll do the same for you when you need him to."

My heart leaps in my chest, acknowledging the truth in her words.

"Okay," I say through a tight throat again.

"Okay, you're going?"

"Yeah, I'm going to go."

"Woohoo!" she shouts, and I have to hold the phone away from my ear with a chuckle.

"I'll have to find someone to sublet our place, and I have a whole bunch of legal paperwork to get finished with Beck to sell him On Pointe. I'm going to need a massive to do list."

"Sweetie, get your butt on a plane today. You can always come back to tie up loose ends, but you need to go to your man and tell him you're not letting him get away."

"Yeah," I agree. "Okay, yeah. I love you Mom. Thank you for talking some sense into me."

"Anytime. I love you, have a safe flight, and call me in a few days to tell me how happy you are."

"I will."

CHAPTER 26

Max

I drag myself up the stairs to my apartment after a long ass day. I can't wait to crawl into bed and call Clay. The only thing that would be better would be if Clay was here with me, so I could touch him, kiss him, and reassure myself that he's still mine.

I stop short when I notice someone sitting in the hallway, leaning against my apartment door.

I blink a few times, refusing to believe my eyes.

"Clay?" I ask, praying I'm not wrong.

He turns his head and smiles, and my heart swells.

"Max," he says, climbing to his feet.

"Holy shit," I breathe before sprinting toward him and pulling my man into my arms. His small body fits against mine just as I remembered, and he smells even better than ever. "What are you doing here?"

Clay opens his mouth to answer, but I can't resist pressing my lips to his, savoring his taste. I lick into his mouth, and we both moan.

"Let's go inside," Clay suggest breathlessly.

I reluctantly set him down and fish my keys out of my pocket. As soon as we're inside and the door is closed behind us, I scoop him up again and beeline for my bedroom.

"I fucking missed you," I murmur against the sweet skin on his throat. I can't stop kissing, nipping, gorging myself on his flavor. "I need you so badly, petal."

"I need you too, baby."

I drop Clay onto my bed and waste no time getting him undressed. With his bindings packed away in my closet, I make use of his shirt to secure his hands to my headboard. And then I lick my way across the smooth plains of his chest and stomach. I know he likes when I edge him for hours, but I'm too impatient right now for that.

"I promise I'll take care of you so good later, but right now I need to get inside you."

"Yes, please Max," Clay agrees with a whimper.

I shed my own clothes and then reach for the lube on my nightstand. Good thing I needed it for jerking off, otherwise we'd be shit out of luck.

I return to Clay, spread out and bound to my bed, his breath coming out in short pants and his skin beautifully flushed.

I cover his body with mine and devour his mouth again. I'll never get enough of the feel of his skin against mine or his scent surrounding me. I want to get lost in every part of him. I want to make Clay shake and cry out with ecstasy.

"Please get inside me," he begs, before sucking my bottom lip between his teeth.

I coat my fingers with lube and slide them between his cheeks, over his quivering hole. He's so tight and so perfect as I slide my middle finger inside slowly. Clay bucks his hips, but I maintain a steady pace as I stretch him open to take me. I add a second finger, slicking his insides.

"Are you ready for me, petal?"

"Yes," he breathes with desperation.

I use the remainder of the lube to coat my throbbing cock and then position myself against his hot entrance.

"Tell me you're mine," I plead as I steadily press inside.

"God, I'm yours; I've always been yours. I love you," Clay babbles as I pop through the tight ring of muscles, and his hole sucks me deep.

"I love you," I reply, my voice tight with restraint as I bottom out inside my man.

"Don't be gentle," Clay gasps, bucking his hips to encourage me.

I pull out and slam home, and we both let out relieved cries. I repeat the motion, fucking into him hard and fast. Clay's head tips back, his mouth falling open as I set a punishing pace.

His cock rubs against my abs, leaving me sticky with his pre-cum. I claim his mouth again without slowing my thrusts, and he returns my kiss with fervor.

His body starts to tremble against mine as I push his legs higher, so I can hit his prostate with every thrust.

"*Ohgodyes,*" he cries out, and then he tenses. His already tight channel clamps down around me, and a groan tears from my throat at the unholy pleasure he draws from me. My balls pull up tight, and I empty myself deep inside him as his release paints my stomach.

What feels like an eternity of pleasure later, I roll off Clay and tug his hands free of the makeshift binding. Then, I pull him into my arms.

"I can't believe you're here," I whisper.

"I'm staying," he replies.

"You're what?" I ask, not daring to believe he means what I hope he does.

"I'm staying. I'm going to sell On Pointe to Beck. I'll have to go home one more time and pack up all my stuff."

"Yeah, I didn't see a suitcase or anything. Where's your stuff?"

"I couldn't wait. I missed you too much. I decided a few hours ago I had to see you, and I got on the first flight out here."

"And you're staying?"

"If you still want me, of course."

"Still want you?" I laugh incredulously. "Petal, there will never be a moment when my heart is beating that I don't want you. Don't you dare ever doubt that."

"I love you, Max."

"I don't know how I got so lucky, but god, I love you so much, Clay." I kiss his cheeks and his nose, then his lips. "We should get married," I blurt.

"What?" Clay asks, drawing in a sharp breath. "You're not serious?"

"Hell yeah, I'm serious. I don't have a ring or any-thing, so I'll have to do this properly another day. But I want you for the rest of my life. Please, be my husband?"

"Yes!" Clay climbs on top of me kisses me long and deep until we're both breathless.

I can't believe I almost missed out on all of this. If I'd been too afraid to explore these feelings, I would've gone the rest of my life never knowing what it's like to love and be loved by my best friend.

"You're the best thing that's ever happened to me," I say against his lips.

"Back at you, love."

COMING SOON!

Inked in Vegas (A Heathens Ink Novella)

An outrageous scavenger hunt, an unexpected trip to the altar, and a wild night with an ex-boyfriend. What happens in Vegas stays in Vegas...right?

Join the Heathens crew as they hit Sin City to celebrate the upcoming nuptials of Madden and Thane, you know these men never do anything half-assed.

Excerpt:

CHAPTER 1

Madden

"I'm looking at them right now and they say: 'Jane and Madden Forever'."

"And that's incorrect?" The woman on the other end of the phone asks in an infuriatingly calm voice.

"Yes, that is incorrect," I snap. "I don't know who the hell Jane is, I'm sure she's a lovely woman, but I'm marrying a *man* named *Th*-ane. Say it with me sweetie...T.H.A.N.E." I admit I may be bordering on hysterical, but it's eight freaking days before my wedding and the programs say Jane and Madden. Who the fuck is *Jane*?

"Okay sir, I understand. I'll get the corrected programs shipped straight to you."

"Thank you, but our wedding is in eight days. That's one week from tomorrow. They'll be here in time, won't they?"

Before I can hear her reassurances, my phone is snagged out of my hand.

"Thank you very much, we appreciate it. You have a lovely day," Thane says in a smooth voice before hanging up my phone and putting it in his own pocket. "You need to relax, sweetheart.

I hate to say it but you've turned into a bit of a groomzilla."

"You don't understand," I say, trying not to slip into a full-on pout.

I just want to make our wedding perfect, so I can show Thane how much I love him and how deeply I appreciate his patience with me when I was struggling so hard to cope. I acted like a complete dick early on in our relationship and maybe if I can give him the most perfect wedding in the history of human civilization it will make up for it. He deserves a perfect wedding and so much more.

"What I understand is there's no reason for this much stress. All I care about is getting to call you mine for the rest of our lives. I already told you, I'd be more than happy to tie the knot in Vegas this weekend during our bachelor party."

I gasp in indignation, even though this isn't news to me.

"After all this planning you'd better believe we are having a damn wedding next weekend come hell or high water."

"Whatever makes you happy," Thane says before pulling me in for a slow, sweet kiss.

Most days I can't believe this incredible man wants to spend the rest of his life with me. I've faced down my fair share of demons in my life, and even more so in the last year and a half, and now that I'm safely on the other side of those nightmares my life doesn't feel real, in the best possible way.

"*You* make me happy," I tell him between kisses.

"I bet I can make you even happier," Thane teases, fingers finding their way to my button fly.

As if on cue there's a loud knock on the front door and we both groan in frustration.

"That must be Royal, Nash, and Zade. Guess this will have to wait," I lament, stroking Thane through his jeans.

"Can't we make them wait? If anyone would understand it'll be those guys," Thane argues.

I laugh and give Thane one more kiss before wiggling out of his arms and heading for the front door.

When I pull the door open I'm not surprised to find Royal and Zade rough-housing while Nash stands between them looking thoroughly harassed.

"This is going to be such a long weekend," he complains as Zade and Royal shout 'Vegas Baby' in concert.

"By the way, Dani's running late. She texted to tell me she went to the store and ran into Beau and lost track of time. She'll meet us at the airport, though."

"I thought she was over that crush after they finally hooked up," I muse.

"Beau is definitely worthy of an encore. Trust me, you guys *want* to see him naked. So fucking hot," Royal fans himself dramatically.

"Hey," Nash complains.

"What can I say, I'm partial to long hair and tattoos," Royal defends, looking Nash up and down pointedly.

"Hey," Zade complains this time.

"Oh my god, you guys. I think you're both sexy as hell, no one compares to either of you," Royal amends in a put-upon tone.

"Too late to make it up to us now. To punish you Nash and I will be joining the mile high club without you," Zade teases.

I laugh and shake my head at their antics. I've always been a little skeptical about how poly relationships work, but spending a few minutes with Nash, Royal, and Zade it's easy to see that they simply fit together. I'm sure any two of them could be happy as a couple, but the three of them complete each other.

"Are you guys ready to go, or did you need a few more minutes?" Nash asks.

"We're ready," Thane says, appearing behind me with our suitcases.

"Let's do this!" Royal exclaims, throwing his hands in the air and dancing around excitedly.

MORE HEATHENS INK

➢ Missed Thane and Madden's full story? Get it here

➢ Dying to know how Royal, Zade, and Nash got together? Get it here

➢ Curious about Adam and Nox's story? Click here

➢ Want to find out how Beck put Gage's shattered heart back together? Click here

➢ Are you a major masochist who *really* wants to get a glimpse into Johnny's heart and mind before he died? You're in luck, grab the FREE novella here

MORE BY K.M.NEUHOLD

➢ <u>Love porn stars? Check out the epic collaboration between K.M. and Nora Phoenix!</u> <u>Get a free prequel to their brand new series,</u> <u>and the first book now!</u>

- ✓ Click Here for Ballsy (A Ballsy Boys Prequel)
- ✓ Click Here for Rebel (Ballsy Boys, 1)

ABOUT THE AUTHOR

Author K.M.Neuhold is a complete romance junkie, a total sap in every way. She started her journey as an author in new adult, MF romance, but after a chance reading of an MM book she was completely hooked on everything about lovely- and sometimes damaged- men finding their Happily Ever After together. She has a strong passion for writing characters with a lot of heart and soul, and a bit of humor as well. And she fully admits that her OCD tendencies of making sure every side character has a full backstory will likely always lead to every book having a spin-off or series. When she's not writing she's a lion tamer, an astronaut, and a superhero...just kidding, she's likely watching Netflix and snuggling with her husky while her amazing husband brings her coffee.

STALK ME

Webisite: kmneuhold@weebly.com

Twitter: @KMNeuhold

Join my Mailing List for special bonus scenes and teasers!

Facebook reader group- Neuhold's Nerds You want to be here, we have crazy amounts of fun

Printed in Great Britain
by Amazon